The President's Secret

Martin Kurzer

outskirtspress
DENVER, COLORADO

Outskirts Press, Inc.
http://www.outskirtspress.com

ISBN: 978-1-4327-9707-2

Outskirts Press and the "OP" logo are trademarks belonging to Outskirts Press, Inc.

PRINTED IN THE UNITED STATES OF AMERICA

This book is dedicated to
Joy Kurzer,
Jodi Kurzer and
Cheryl Broder.
You are always in my thoughts.

Preface

On March 26, 2012, Reuters News Service reported that United States President Barak Obama was caught on-camera in Seoul assuring outgoing Russian President Dmitry Medvedev that he will have "more flexibility" to deal with contentious issues such as missile defense after the U.S. presidential election. Obama asked Moscow to give him "space" until after the November election in which Obama was running for re-election as President of the United States. The two of them were unaware that their discussion was being picked up on microphones. Obama's Republican opponents have accused him of being too open to concessions to the Russians on the issue of the U.S. planned anti-missile shield.

Obama told Medvedev that he needed time "particularly with missile defense" until he is in a better position politically to resolve such issues. Medvedev responded that "I understand your message about space." Obama added: "This is my last election...After my election I have more flexibility." Medvedev promised to "transmit this information to Vladimir" Putin, the power behind Medvedev and Russia's incoming president.

In effect, Obama was telling the Russians that caving in to them on the missile defense issue was a political football that might hurt his run for re-election and that he could only do so after the election since, once he is re-elected, he can do whatever he wants because he will be ineligible to run again.

A few months earlier, Obama was also overheard by the press telling the President of France that he strongly dislikes Israel's chief,

Benjamin Netanyahu but that he has to deal with him every day.

Although this book is a piece of fiction I began writing before Obama's first gaffe with the French and it was mostly finished before the news of his conversation with Medvedev was released, strangely the two Obama meetings that were overheard by the press fit very closely the basis for my story. So, perhaps truth is stranger than fiction, or at least, in this case, perhaps fiction may predict the future truth. On this point, I leave the reader to his or her own conclusion.

Chapter 1

It was the most unusual day in Robert Johnson's life. The forecast for Washington, D.C. on that Tuesday was sunny and warm. So far as Robert knew, it would be a boring day like most of his days.

What Robert did not yet know when he slid out of bed at 5:00AM was that the day would change, and probably considerably shorten, his life. That Tuesday would present him with a unique opportunity and give him choices he had never before dreamed about. Along with the opportunity, however, was a danger he never even imagined.

Robert would have a decision to make on that fateful Tuesday. That decision would affect not just Robert, but also the world. By the time Robert recognized the danger that accompanied the opportunity, it would be too late to halt the forces that he had unknowingly set in motion.

Chapter 2

Robert slowly headed for the bathroom. Once there, he casually stretched and removed his red pajamas. He liked red pajamas. In fact, he liked the color red in general. Red, he thought, was a power color, and he felt powerful when he wore red. After all, Robert reasoned, during the presidential debates, the candidates usually wore a dark suit, a white shirt, and a red tie. Yes, it was the red tie that gave all of them that look of power. If it was a good enough color for presidential candidates, it was certainly good enough for Robert.

Robert set the shower to be nice and hot. That hot water opened his pores and made him feel completely relaxed. After a few minutes under that hot water, Robert toweled off and got dressed. He put on a nondescript grey uniform, but, in Robert's mind there were two things about it that made him feel important. First, he tucked a red handkerchief into the left breast pocket. Second, and even more important, was the script sewn several inches above that pocket: "The White House" and just below that "Sanitary Engineer." Robert made sure that the red handkerchief never covered any part of that script.

Breakfast was made up of grits, fried eggs, and a sliced tomato washed down with three cups of black coffee. He really liked sausages and bacon, but his doctor recently told him to cut down on those fats. So, sausages and bacon were now relegated to the weekend as a special treat.

When breakfast was over, Robert brushed his teeth, combed his hair, and looked into the mirror. He smiled and headed out to his pride and joy, his 1988 5-series red BMW. It burned a lot of gas, but man could that car corner and accelerate. Along with its red color, that car strongly added to his feeling of power. He opened the door, and sat in the still beautiful leather seats. Then he turned the key in the ignition, the machine roared to life, and he was on his way to work at the White House.

Robert parked in his special place and moved through security, waving to the guards and chatting as he headed to the closet that held his cleaning equipment. If he was lucky, he might catch a glimpse of the president or the first lady. That happened every now and then. Occasionally the president might nod to him, but the president had no idea who Robert was. Though neither the president nor Robert yet knew it, that was soon going to change.

Every mop, every duster, every cleaning towel, and every rolling pail had the White House logo emblazoned on it. It was impressive, and Robert stuffed a towel under his shirt every once in a while and took it home. Since it was morning, cleaning was limited to dusting and wiping. Mopping was left for the evening when most people were gone. Robert grabbed a duster and a supply of towels, put them into a rolling cart, and headed out on his designated rounds. Today was Tuesday, so he would begin by cleaning the president's private media/conference room in the basement and then move to the first floor offices. Cleaning the media/conference room made Robert feel as if he worked directly for the president, so he liked to begin his day that way.

Chapter 3

President J. Washington Rock quickly stood up and got out of his chair. He was a man on a mission and he looked intense. He picked up the sheaf of papers from his desk and sighed. He was as ready as he would ever be. This would be his time, his defining moment. One false word could mean disaster to his re-election dreams, but he was certain that he would be flawless.

The president bounded to the door with determination. He opened the door and headed to a nearby office and knocked on the door.

"It is time," he said.

"I know and I am ready," came the reply.

The door opened and out came the first lady. She squeezed his hand and smiled. He put his arm through hers.

"Let's go," he said.

As they walked down the hall, they were joined by two senior staffers who were very close to the president. Only the four of them and the president's confidential secretary, who had typed the presentation, were aware of the existence of the meeting, and even the staffers did not know the content of the presentation.

When they reached the door of the president's small, private media room, one of the staffers opened the door and the four of them walked in. The staffers sat in the back. The president and the first lady sat next to the podium at the front of the room. The president wanted to be present to greet each guest as he arrived. Protocol was very important to those people, and they were not to be kept waiting.

The president glanced at his watch and nodded to the staffers. They nodded back and immediately left the room, heading to a small rear door at the White House. That door was only used for special guests who were not to be seen by reporters and the general public. Today's guests were to be seen by no one if at all possible. This meeting was so secret that the guests were to arrive at staggered times, with no two arriving at the same time.

Within a few minutes they began to arrive, escorted to the media room by the staffers. Some were in business suits, but most were in the middle eastern dress of sheiks. The president and the first lady greeted each of them and invited them to sit down. Appropriate food and refreshments were available on a nearby table.

There were high ranking representatives of Morocco, Algeria, Tunisia, Libya, Egypt, Lebanon, Sudan, Syria, Jordan, Iraq, Saudi Arabia, Kuwait, Bahrain, Qatar, U.A.E., Oman, and Yemen. Even Iran sent a representative. The president thought of inviting the Russians because he believed that his plan would be well accepted by them, but he did not trust their government and he could not risk having the details of his presentation leak out.

After all of the guests had finished their refreshments and taken their seats, the president rose to begin, but before he could start he noticed some movement behind the soundproof glass in the media area of the room. He immediately sent a staffer to remove whoever was back there.

Robert Johnson was in the process of cleaning and dusting the media area when the staffer came in and told him to leave and return to finish his cleaning in a couple of hours. As Robert picked up one of his dustcloths, he inadvertently touched a button on the media control panel. Neither he nor the staffer noticed the small green light that came on. The staffer walked with Robert until Robert was out of the room. The staffer then closed the door and returned to his seat in the rear of the room.

Now the president smiled and began.

"Hello everyone. I am sure you want to know why I have invited you here. Probably the most surprised person of all to be invited is the delegate from Iran. I promised each of your governments that it would be well worth your time to attend this meeting, and now I am going to deliver on that promise. We have been perceived as an enemy of Iran, and of Islam, and a friend of the mortal enemy of many of your governments, Israel. Well, that perception is going to change as soon as I am re-elected."

The delegates stirred in their seats, leaning forward to listen more closely as the president continued.

"You see, I have always considered bringing peace to the Middle East and, as a result of that, to most of the world, to be not only my goal, but also my legacy to the world. I want peace and understanding between the nations of the Middle East and the United States. I no longer want the United States to be known as the Great Satan in the Middle East. I want you and your governments to think of the United States as your friend.

"So how am I going to create this peaceful world? Of course, it will take your help. So what can I do to earn your trust? I can give you something each and every one of you wants, something you have fought wars to achieve—the downfall of Israel."

That last statement resulted in considerable rustling in the room as well as astonished looks from the delegates toward each other.

President Rock smiled and continued.

"I believe that all of the problems between your countries and the United States can be traced to the creation of Israel."

A few heads nodded affirmatively.

"Some of your governments want a negotiated settlement between the Palestinians and Israel, and others simply refuse to make peace with Israel under any circumstances. I am not here to judge who is right and who is wrong. I am here to solve the problem. Oh yes, there is a solution!

"It is clear that there will never be a negotiated settlement between the Palestinians and Israel. Many years ago, Israel offered just about everything except the right of return to Israel. Of course, agreeing to the unlimited right of return of displaced Palestinians to Israel would have destroyed Israel, so I can understand why it was not offered. Anyway, Arafat rejected the offer without even a counteroffer, thus creating the present holy war with Israel. The result is that the present Israeli and Palestinian governments are much farther from peace than they have been in many years. As I said before, I am not here to judge who is right and who is wrong. I am here to solve the problem and bring peace between the Arab countries of the Middle East and the United States. You have undoubtedly noticed that there is no representative of Israel here.

"So here is my solution. If and when I am re-elected to my second term as President of the United States, I will do everything in my power—and I can do a considerable amount—to end the economic and military aid of the United States to Israel."

The delegates turned to each other in disbelief.

"Oh yes, I am quite serious. You must have noticed that I have been to many of your countries, but that I have never set foot on Israeli soil as president of the United States. The fact is that I do not particularly like Jews in general, and in particular I hate the Israeli government. The Israelis are pushy and demanding, while I think of myself as friendly. Thus, I simply don't like them.

"Yes, I know what you are thinking: 'Then why do I have some Jews in my cabinet and why haven't I cut off aid to Israel in the past?' The answer to both questions is the same—I need Jewish campaign contributions and Jewish votes to be re-elected. Therefore, I have to appear to be a friend of Israel and of American Jews until I am re-elected.

"This will be my second term as president of the United states. Our constitution does not allow me to run for a third term. So, when I am re-elected, I will be a lame-duck president and I can do things that will be very unpopular to American Jews and other American pro-Israel groups because I will no longer need their money or their votes. Basically, I will have Israel between this Rock and a hard place."

The room erupted in laughter. When it died down, President Rock continued.

"Now, here is what I need from you in order to help me to be re-elected so that I can carry out what I have just promised to you.

"First, I need you to immediately tone down your anti-United States rhetoric. Instead, I want you to slowly begin to have your governments say a few nice things about me and to invite me for a brief visit. That will help to get votes because I will be perceived by voters as someone who can make peace between your countries and the United States. That is very important to me because most Americans desire peace. I want you to do this slowly because if you make large or rapid changes in our relationship, some people will question why.

"Second, I would appreciate any funds you can contribute to my re-election campaign. That should be done carefully and through United States companies, trusts, and individuals. I do not want funds coming in from foreign entities.

"The third, and probably most important, thing I need from you is absolute silence about the nature of this meeting. My promise to you at this meeting is to be repeated only at the highest levels of your governments and only on a need to know basis. If word of this meeting leaks out, I will lose my Jewish voter and contribution base, and I will probably lose the election.

"If I lose, you lose. Can I count on your support?"

Every Middle East delegate stood and applauded. President Rock smiled broadly and shook hands with each delegate. Then the delegates departed through the back door one at a time, so as not to call attention to themselves. When all of them were gone, President Rock pounded his right fist into his left palm with a loud smack.

"I've done it," he said.

Meanwhile outside, a short, muscular man stood scanning the

street and the roofs at the rear of the White House. None of the delegates was to leave while anyone was in the area. He stood in the shadows and kept well out of sight. Everything remained quiet for a long time. Just as the last delegate was leaving, perhaps by intuition, because he was very skilled and experienced at his craft, he felt that someone was watching. He scanned the roofs again with his binoculars. At first everything seemed to be clear. Then he noticed a very small movement on the top of a nearby roof.

The man moved quickly toward that building and then bounded rapidly up the back stairs to the roof. There was an elevator, but he used the stairs very quietly to avoid being noticed. When he reached the door to the roof, he was hardly breathing hard. All of his gym time was paying off.

The man slowly and quietly opened the door to the roof and stepped through it. He stopped, but he heard nothing. He removed the 45 from his shoulder holster. He very quietly moved to his left around the chimney. Still nothing.

When he had moved nearly all the way around the chimney, he finally saw what had attracted his attention. It was a young boy with a camera. The man replaced the 45 into his holster and walked up to the boy.

"Hi, I'm Peter. What is your name, young man?"

"Hi, my name is Rory."

"Well what in the world are you doing way up here, Rory?"

"Today is my twelfth birthday and my parents gave me this camera for a present. This is just the camera I really wanted. It uses real film, not like the modern ones they sell today. Dad had a lot of trouble finding this one."

Really. Have you been taking pictures?"

"Oh yes. I've been taking lots of pictures of very interesting men coming out of the back door of the White House. Some of them were even dressed up as sheiks. Some of them even looked up as they came out, and I got good pictures of their faces with my zoom lens."

"How interesting. Can I see your camera?"

Rory handed over the camera with a big smile. Peter seemed so interested in what Rory was doing.

Peter looked at the camera. His orders were clear. He knew what he had to do. He said: "Happy Birthday." Then, with a short, powerful push of his right hand, he shoved Rory over the edge. He didn't want to push too hard because he wanted Rory to fall near the building so that it appeared that Rory had just leaned over too far instead of being pushed.

Rory felt as if he were flying, except that he had no wings. He suddenly realized what was happening. He let out a short scream just before he splattered into the ground.

Peter opened the camera. It had no film. "Too bad," Peter thought, "the kid died for nothing, and on his birthday no less. Oh well." He placed the camera carefully next to the ledge.

Peter could already hear the ambulance sirens as he moved rapidly and silently down the stairs and out of the door. He knew that no ambulance could help Rory now.

Peter disappeared down the street.

Chapter 4

Chaim Gol looked out of his office window in Jerusalem and shrugged. It sure was hot out there and rain clouds had begun to cover the horizon. A short, stocky man in his mid-60's, Gol didn't look like much, but he was an expert in Israeli intelligence, and he was really excellent at his job.

Gol was born in Germany just after the end of World War II. His parents had managed to get to London before Hitler started murdering Jews in earnest, and they had been among the first Jews to return to Germany after the war. Gol quickly became fluent in both German and English. After the family moved to Israel when he was 10 years old, he added Hebrew and Yiddish, and learned French later.

Because Gol was born in Germany, he was permitted to train with German intelligence via Israeli intelligence. His connections later made it possible to also work with British and U.S. intelligence. Thus, Gol was very well schooled and well connected for his job.

Chaim had held a number of overt and covert jobs with Israeli intelligence over the years in several different countries. Now, because of his age, he was unhappily relegated to a desk job that he found to be quite boring. He was responsible for the tracking of high ranking government officials of the unfriendly Middle Eastern countries surrounding Israel.

The job was typically pretty routine, but, piecing together information from a number of sources, Chaim noticed a pattern that caught his attention. A number of the people he was routinely tracking from several different countries suddenly disappeared around the same time. That had never happened before. Even more surprising was that two of them were spotted in Washington, D.C. at the same time.

Chaim wondered what the hell was going on.

Picking up a secure phone, he called a secure connection at the Israeli Embassy in Washington, D.C. After ringing twice, the chief of intelligence at the embassy answered.

"George Boles speaking. What can I do for you?"

"This is Gol. I need your help."

"Yes, Mr. Gol. How can I help you?'

"I understand that two Middle East high ranking officials have just arrived in your town. I want to know where they are staying, where they have been, where they go, and how and when they leave. I need to know that yesterday. Clear?"

I'll get right on that and call you back."

Leaning back in his chair, Gol pondered the possibilities. It was probably nothing, but it was best to be safe. About three hours later, his secure phone rang.

"Mr. Gol, this is George Boles. I think something may be going on here."

"Yes?"

"Both of them are staying at the Washington Hilton, though on different floors. They both checked in yesterday. Through some bribes and connections, we discovered that they had dinner together with a third man in the hotel coffee shop on the day they arrived."

It turned out that the third man was another of the missing people Gol was tracking. Now his interest was really piqued.

"Continue."

"The next morning, all three of them headed in the direction of the White House about five minutes apart, and they all returned to the hotel about two hours later, again about five minutes apart. What the hell do you think is happening?"

"I don't know yet and maybe we will never find out. Keep me posted on all of their movements and anyone who seems connected to them. Whatever your men do, don't let them get spotted."

"Yes sir."

Gol hung the phone up. He picked up the phone and dialed his assistant.

"Did you notice the reports of all of those Middle East hot shots who disappeared from our radar screen around the same time?"

"Yes. What do think is going on?"

"I'm not sure, but three of them have turned up in Washington, D.C. I'm having all of them tracked."

"Whew."

"Increase coverage immediately on everyone who is missing. Also, I want every access point in those countries watched 24/7 until we find these guys. If any of them returns from out of the country, I want to know when, how, who they arrived with, and where they came from, as well as anything else you can find out. One other thing–I don't want anyone to know that we want to know. That's crucial."

"Will do."

Gol hung up. Then he picked up the phone again and hit the intercom button.

"Get me the Prime Minister."

Gol's phone quickly rang. The voice at the other end told him that the Prime Minister would speak to him immediately.

" Chaim, what is so important?"

"It may be nothing, Mr. Prime Minister, but I think it's something. I need to see you right now."

"Come over now. I'll tell my secretary to show you right in."

When Gol arrived, he was immediately shown in to the Prime Minister's office.

"Ok, Chaim, let's have it."

Gol gave the Prime Minister a full briefing.

" Well, well, well. I agree that something is going on, maybe something big involving the U.S. government. But what?"

"I don't know, Mr. Prime Minister."

"Alright. Keep me posted any hour of the day or night. For now there is nothing else to be done except to watch and listen. Good work."

"Yes, sir."

Chaim left for his office. He was very concerned, but the Prime Minister was right that all the situation called for now was to observe.

Chapter 5

When Robert Johnson left the media room, he headed to his other cleaning assignments, where he cleaned and dusted per his usual schedule. Robert was a creature of habit and he would have preferred to clean the media room first. After all, he had never seen anyone use it that early in the morning before. Nevertheless, once he had started on his revised rounds, he forgot all about the media room.

Robert was working his Tuesday schedule, morning and afternoon. Sometimes he worked the afternoon and evening schedule. On those days, the morning man in that part of the building cleaned the media room unless there had been a meeting in it during the day, in which case Robert vacuumed it in the evening and the morning man dusted it the next day.

So, Robert went on his revised rounds on that Tuesday. Sometimes he spent part of his lunch time talking to one of the secretaries. On this Tuesday, he decided to visit with one of his favorites, Carol Norman, the secretary to one of President Rock's junior staffers, John Davis. Robert had never met Davis, but talking to Carol was usually entertaining.

Robert marched into Carol's office just after he finished the sandwich he had brought from home. His girl friend, Shirley Stevens, had made the fried egg and cheese sandwich the night before and left it in the refrigerator for him along with a nice supply of olives and shaved carrots. That, thought Robert, was a tasty lunch and he had washed it down with two cups of coffee from the cafeteria which made it even better.

When Robert arrived at Carol's office, she was just beginning to relax after her cafeteria lunch.

"Well, Robert, how nice to see you today."

"I've cleaned faster than usual today, so I thought I'd kill a few minutes with one of my favorite people, you."

"How flattering. By the way, do you ever intend to marry that girlfriend of yours?"

"I've told you before that I really like her, but why should I ruin a great relationship by marrying her?"

"Oh Robert, you're terrible. Give the poor girl a break."

They both laughed.

"Seriously, Carol, let me change the subject to President Rock. Since you work for one of his staffers, what is the inside scoop on the president's chances for re-election?"

"The truth is that I don't have the foggiest idea. Mr. Davis, if he knows anything, has said nothing to me. The president never comes here and I've never even met the man. When he wants Mr. Davis for something, Mr. Davis is called to the president's office or to a conference room. I'm just the local drudge, making and taking phone calls and typing. That's about it. Anything Mr. Davis knows, he keeps to himself.

"Well, if you can't tell me anything important, I might as well go back to work. Oops, I just remembered that I haven't cleaned the media room yet, so I'd better get moving."

Robert shuffled down the hall, picked up his cleaning and dusting supplies, and walked to the media room. He was only required to dust during the day shift, but he saw the mess from the morning meeting and decided to be a good guy and clean it up. He went out and came back with a vacuum cleaner and garbage bags. It took about half an hour to clean the meeting room after which Robert looked at the room and smiled. It looked much better now, Robert thought, because he took pride in his work. Next, he moved to the media area of the room behind the soundproof glass and began dusting.

When Robert began to dust the media control panel, he noticed a small red light blinking. He looked more closely and saw that it was just above the "record" button. He pushed the "stop" button next to it and the red light went out. Robert was pleased with himself because he had only guessed that the "stop" button might work. He wondered what had been recorded, so he pushed the "play" button. He immediately saw a disc begin to turn and then he heard the president's voice.

"Hello everyone. I am sure you want to know why I have invited you here. Probably the most surprised person of all to be invited is the delegate from Iran. I promised each of your governments that it would be well worth your time to attend this meeting, and now I am going to deliver on that promise. We have been perceived as an enemy of Iran and of Islam, and a friend of the mortal enemy of many of your governments, Israel. Well, that perception is going to change as soon as I am re-elected."

Robert sat down and listened to the rest of the CD. When it finished playing, he sat for several minutes in stunned silence. He got up, removed the CD, put it in his pocket, and left the room. He finished cleaning, all the while replaying the president's words in his mind. Robert was not the brightest bulb on the tree, but he was no fool either and he knew that he had something. The question was what should he do with it?

Robert realized that he needed to give this situation some quiet thought, so when he arrived at his apartment, he picked up the phone and called his girlfriend.

"Shirley, I'm really tired tonight. I had a rough day. Don't come over tonight. I'll see you after work tomorrow instead."

"I could make you feel a lot better, and you know how."

Robert smiled.

"I know you can, sweetie, but not tonight."

"Ok, if that's what you want."

"That's what I want, but just for tonight."

Robert hung up the phone and sat in the dark thinking. He wasn't even hungry.

Robert was very conflicted. On one hand, he really liked President Rock and he had no interest in doing anything that would hurt the president's re-election chances. On the other hand, he had found something of real value to the president and he should be rewarded for it. What would be a fair resolution of this issue? After a long time, he hit upon an arrangement that he thought would be fair to both the president and to Robert—a win/win. He would contact John Davis tomorrow since Davis was the only presidential staffer he had any sort of connection with, but he would keep Carol, Davis' secretary, out of the loop.

The next morning, Robert had no problem obtaining a White House Directory and finding the direct phone number for John Davis. He dialed it and Davis answered.

"This is John Davis."

"Mr. Davis, you don't know me and I am not going to tell you my name. I know that you are a staffer for the president and I am going to give you a message for the president."

"Who are you and how did get this phone number?"

"Don't worry about that. Here is the message and I will speak slowly so that you can write it down and get it exactly right. Accuracy will be very important. Tell the president that I have a CD of a meeting that he had yesterday morning in the media room. It begins with: "Hello everyone. I am sure you want to know why I have invited you here." Just so he understands that I have the whole thing, tell him that it ends with: "I've done it." I want the president to know that I am a big supporter of his and I would never sell the CD to anyone who could hurt him even though I am sure that some people would pay many millions to get it. On the other hand, I am not wealthy and I should get something for finding it and giving it to the president. If this information got into the wrong hands, it could cost the president's re-election campaign hundreds of millions of dollars and lots of votes. Because I am a modest man and a strong believer in the president, all I want to give it to the president is three million dollars. That is a real bargain. There are no other copies and I don't intend to make any. This is a one time payment, call it a reward, and you will never hear from me again. I will phone you again tomorrow morning and you can give me the president's answer. Is all of that clear?

"It's very clear although I don't know anything about the meeting you have described. I will pass the message on."

"Excellent."

Robert hung up, smiled, and began his cleaning rounds.

Davis called Carol into his office.

"Carol, have you heard anything about any meetings the president may have had yesterday?"

"Not a word, but I can't think of any reason why I would have heard anything. Do you want me to try to find out?"

"No, no. Just forget about it. It has nothing to do with us anyway."

Carol left the room, closed the door, and returned to her desk. Davis picked up the phone and dialed the president's secretary to set up an appointment with the president as soon as possible.

Chapter 6

Robert Johnson was far less a product of his family upbringing than of his indifference to his own life style. Robert was far from brilliant, but he could have done more with his life than he had thus far. He liked the easy way if at all possible, which is why he decided to take monetary advantage of finding the CD of the president's secret presentation. While President Rock was a risk-taker, Robert went wherever the flow of life took him. That was simply his nature.

Robert was black. At age 36, he stood 5'8" and weighed a flabby 170 pounds. Exercise was not his thing, but he was basically fit from working as a janitor at the White House. When he was not at work, he liked to watch TV and drink beer, though he limited himself to lots of coffee while at work—no drinking on the job. He liked the prestige of working at the White House, and he thought of himself as working for the President of the United States.

While comfortable in his lifestyle, Robert always thought he would like one big financial hit so that he could live like a "somebody." He made $58,000 a year and lived in a nice, but plain apartment, and he was satisfied with his life. In short, he was built for comfort and preferred to wait for a big opportunity to fall into his lap rather than to actively pursue it. As fortune would have it, fortune, in the shape of the president's CD, had now fallen into his lap and he intended to cash in. He had not yet recognized the danger that accompanied that good fortune.

Robert was born in Washington, D.C. to parents who tried to imbue in him some ambition. Unfortunately, he was immune to their efforts. His early school friends were a mixed bag. Two had become lawyers and one was now a doctor, but Robert followed more closely the ones who became store clerks, salesmen, and garbage men. The path he had chosen was an irritant to his parents, but they were happy that none of his friends ended up in jail or worse since they would have worried that their son may have followed that group. There really was no risk of that because he was never wild as a child or adult.

Thomas and Evonne Johnson, Robert's parents, lived a comfortable lifestyle. Unlike their only son, they had many friends, whereas Robert only had his girlfriend, Shirley Stevens. Thomas worked on the line in an automobile assembly plant and Evonne was a secretary in administration at a department store. They generally avoided politics, but they did support President Rock. They enjoyed playing bridge, going to the movies, and going to dinner with friends.

When Robert was not at work, unless he was watching TV, he liked to play, sexually, with Shirley Stevens. He had met Shirley six years ago while she was working as a checkout clerk in a department store. As soon as he saw her, he thought that she was cute and immediately asked her for a date. She was flattered and she accepted. They had been dating ever since.

Standing a chubby 5'3', Shirley was black. She was 28 years old and was fairly attractive with a nice figure that Robert enjoyed fondling. Her family kept bugging her to get rid of Robert and to find a suitable husband. They feared that she would waste her most attractive years on Robert, a basically lazy person who had no intention of marrying her and who had no fiscal future because he drank away his salary in beer. Their evaluation of Robert was pretty much on the mark. Shirley lived with her parents, except when she spent the night at Robert's apartment, so she had to listen to her parents' constant carping. She believed that they may be correct, but she loved Robert and she hoped that he might pop the marriage question someday.

Getting married was something that Robert never intended to do. He did not want a wife and he did not want to take care of crying children. He would lavish presents on Shirley once the president paid him, but marry her? Never.

Chapter 7

When President J. Washington Rock stood, he had a look of importance. He was 6'2", and 230 pounds at age 59. While he was not the first black president, he had a great following among blacks, Jews, and other historically liberal groups because he was black and a Democrat. While he was known as a captivating speaker, he was always much better in front of a teleprompter where he did not have to think under pressure. Without the teleprompter or a professionally written speech, he tended to hem and haw and sometimes let his true views come out, which would probably not help him get re-elected. He certainly embraced socialistic ideas—take from the productive and give to those who were not as talented. Of course, that Robin Hood approach had worked wonderfully in attracting lots of votes for Latin American despots such as Hugo Chavez, and President Rock used the technique well in his initial election since have-nots make up a large portion of the electorate and frequently vote for someone who promises to give them something for nothing. The secret motto of his initial election team was borrowed from an old perfume ad: "Promise them anything, but give them Arpege by Lanvin."

Promising people anything and being as vague as possible certainly worked for Rock. The private joke of his Republican opponent that Rock was no Rock-et scientist may have been accurate, but fell far short of winning. Rock swept to a fairly easy victory.

The run for re-election would likely be a different story. The president had been in office for nearly his first full term, and even the liberals knew that he was ill-equipped mentally to deliver on his initial promises. He sounded great, but he had no real experience at governing before being elected and that showed throughout his first term. Making grand promises might get a candidate elected the first time, but it is necessary to carry most of them out in order to capture those votes the second time around. The perfume Arpege smelled sweeter than some of the president's programs.

Under the circumstances, one might think that Rock would lose his contributor and voter base, but such was not the case. He had one trump card that he would play constantly—always blame someone else: his predecessor in office created the problem and it would take more time to fix it; Congress wouldn't allow him to the fix the mess he had inherited; you name the problem and someone else was responsible for it; the Republicans were out to sabotage his programs; and all attacks on him were racially motivated. His strategy worked pretty well with the liberals and with the liberal press, but independents were not as convinced. Thus, he faced a tough re-election campaign.

J. Washington Rock was born in Detroit, Michigan to parents who were involved in the civil rights movement. Although they were college educated and marched with Jews who had died for the cause, they became neutral on Jews after the black community blamed Jews for being slum lords. They didn't hate Jews; they just didn't care whether Jews lived or died. Their only son was raised with this apathy to Jews and their causes.

As he grew older, he hung out with people who were outspoken critics of Jews in general and Israel in particular. Many of his oldest friends, spiritual advisers, and confidants were well-known anti-semites. Nevertheless, Jewish voters strongly supported Rock the first time around and were poised to so do again for his re-election, thus ignoring the old adage that the fruit does not fall far from the tree.

In fact, Rock had been strongly influenced by his friends. He genuinely neither liked nor trusted Jews. He was even more influenced by his wife, Rhonda, who resented Jews from an early age. Thus, although President Rock did his best to hide his bias in public, the chips were always going to be stacked against Israel during his presidency. The Israeli government and Israeli public understood this quite well, but it was somehow lost on the vast majority of American Jews.

From the outset of Rock's emergence on the presidential campaigning circuit, the Israeli media and Israeli government early on found the disturbing truth about the anti-Jewish attitudes of Rock's closest friends. Therefore, so as not to be caught unawares by his actions should he be elected, the Israeli government turned to a specialist within one of its security departments.

Mark Corman specialized in behavioral patterns. Corman was born in the United States, where he attended college majoring in psychology at the University of California at Santa Cruz. That campus was an early center for a new field of psychology called Neuro-Linguistic Programming, or NLP. NLP had been created there before Corman attended the school, but many of its top teachers still lived and worked in the Santa Cruz area. Thus, he became interested in NLP and was able to study directly with several of its creators and innovators, and he became a Certified Master Practitioner of NLP. A native of Milwaukee, Mark blended his midwestern no-nonsense form of logical thinking with his NLP training to become a quiet powerhouse in analyzing patterns that were so subtle even the individual himself or herself did not notice them.

When Mark met an Israeli girl studying at the University of California at Santa Cruz, he married her and took his expertise to Israel. He applied to work for the Israeli government, displayed his special observational talents, and ended up in Israeli intelligence.

NLP was created as a modeling technique. It was originally used to notice and map both the internal and external patterns of high achieving persons so that the same patterns could be successfully taught to and used by others. Since many of the original persons modeled were psychologists, NLP morphed into a field of psychology by mapping and teaching the patterns of the best psychologists.

NLP practitioners were highly trained to notice differences in the speaking, postural, and eye movement patterns of the person they were observing. So, after observing someone for a short time, a skilled NLP practitioner could tell to a high degree of certainty when the person was lying. Mark Corman was very good at that.

When Rock was running for president for the first time, the Israeli government assigned Corman to observe and analyze Rock's video archived speeches and interviews. They particularly wanted to know whether Rock was sincere when he claimed to be a friend and supporter of Israel. What Corman discovered left no room for doubt—Rock had simply lied . He would be no friend of Israel.

Mark reported his findings to his chief. The problem was that if Israel leaked this information and Rock was subsequently elected as President of the United States, the political fallout for Israel could be devastating. Israel could lose the support of the liberals she enjoyed in Congress. Thus, it was decided to keep Mark Corman's work confidential. In fact, as president, J. Washington Rock did just enough for Israel to permit Rock to hold on to Jewish support.

Rhonda Billings met Rock at Georgetown, where she studied Education. She was now 55 years old, stood 5'5', and weighed 180 pounds. While she was never a beauty, she carried an outward air of self-confidence that attracted the young Rock to her. He already held a general B.S. from the University of Pittsburgh and was studying law at Georgetown when a mutual friend fixed them up on a date. Rhonda was born in Memphis to parents in the professions. Her father was a CPA and her mother was a teacher.

Rhonda saw that while Rock was not a great thinker, he had a good physical stature and a deep voice. She believed that she could easily control him and train him to do great things. Since at that time a woman could not realistically aspire to be a business leader, he gave her what she wanted—a man who could front for her ambitions. With that in mind, she married him.

After they were married, she taught in inner-city schools, where she blamed whites for the poor education of black children. Rhonda was a highly opinionated fighter and an outspoken critic of the establishment. She was ruthless in her dealings with other people and could smile to one's face while stabbing that person in the back.

Rhonda trained her husband well in her brand of hatred as well to become a good speaker. He learned well enough to first work for the State Department before being elected to Congress from Michigan. After two terms in Congress and with continued tutoring by his wife, some Democratic party bigwigs decided that he was a great speaker and encouraged him to run in the primaries for president even though he had done nothing in Congress to distinguish himself. His wife believed that the less he took a position by voting or saying anything, the less likely he was to give his opponents anything to use against him.

Throughout the primaries, he climbed up the Democratic polls by speaking in broad generalities and promising whatever Rhonda determined to be most likely to garner votes at the time. He soon became the Democratic front-runner since he had no voting record that could be criticized and said nothing of substance. He presented a great platform as long as no one thought about it too hard.

J. Washington Rock wrapped up the Democratic nomination well before the convention. His convention speech was again devoid of a meaningful platform, but no one cared because he was a great speaker and had no baggage that was easy to criticize. With that kind of background, the party powers were confident of victory in November. All that was needed was to add the promise to take from the rich and give to the less fortunate. The votes of the have-nots would be enough to put Rock into the White House.

The strategy worked. J. Washington Rock became President Rock and Rhonda became part of the establishment she had loathed all of her life.

Chapter 8

John Davis quickly climbed the stairs on his way to President Rock's office. His phone call to Josephine, the president's secretary, requesting an immediate audience with "The Boss" was not well received, but when he asked whether there had been a presidential meeting yesterday morning in the media room, he was invited to come immediately.

Even before John got there, Josephine told the president that he had inquired about the meeting for which she had typed his speech. That was a meeting nobody outside of a few people was supposed to know about, and John Davis was not one of those people. President Rock screamed to Josephine "Get his ass in here immediately." She told him that she had already invited Davis to see the president. Rock smiled and sat down to wait.

The wait was not long. Davis was quickly shown into the presidential office where President Rock greeted him warmly.

"Come in , John."

"Thank you, Mr. President."

"Why do you want to see me? There was a meeting yesterday morning about re-election strategy, but it was supposed to be kept confidential because I don't trust the Republicans; they could try to infiltrate it somehow. How did you find out about it?"

"Maybe the Republicans taped it."

"I don't understand."

"I got a strange phone call this morning mentioning the meeting, giving a very specific message for you, and asking for three million dollars."

Davis then proceeded to read the notes he had taken of Robert's phone call. The president listened carefully. His smile hid his anger and deep concern.

"John, as I said, there was a strategy meeting yesterday. I don't know what this person thinks he has or how he got it, but it certainly isn't worth anything close to three million dollars. Do you have any idea who this blackmailer is, because demanding money for information is blackmail."

"I have no idea who he is or how he got my name and phone number."

"Alright, just forget it, and give me your notes. I think this was a crank call, but if he calls you again tell him that I will pay the money if he gives you payment instructions. Then we can catch him and turn him over to the police."

"Yes sir, and I will keep you posted."

"Do that. I want to catch this idiot, so phone my secretary anytime he contacts you."

John left and returned to his office, but he continued to have a nagging thought that maybe there was more to this than the president let on. By the time he got to his office, he put his curiosity in the back of his mind and dug into the pile of work on his desk. Whatever was going on, it had nothing to do with him so there was no reason to worry about it.

As soon as Davis left the president's office and closed the door behind him, President Rock flew into a rage. He buzzed Josephine's intercom.

"Dammit, I want my inner security team and my wife in my office RIGHT NOW! Is that clear?"

"Yes sir, immediately."

She quickly located them, told them the president is in a rage, and to get to his office as quickly as possible." She had rarely seen him raging, so this must be very important. She knew that President Rock had a temper, but it was usually well concealed.

The inner security team arrived first followed closely by Mrs. Rock. The team was headed by Peter, who had proven his worth by dealing with the boy who had seen too much on the morning of the meeting. The president read John Davis's notes of Robert's phone call.

"I want to know how this scheming bastard got a CD of that meeting. I certainly didn't authorize anyone to tape it. I want to know who this guy is and I want to know right now! Next, what do we do about him? The money he is asking for is a drop in the bucket, so we could just pay him off. Since he said he likes me and he has asked for much less than he could get for the CD elsewhere, he would probably keep his word and go away. What do all of you think?"

Peter said: "You are probably right, but there is always some risk in paying off blackmailers. Even if he intends to simply go away and say nothing, he could change his mind later."

Rhonda finally spoke up: "Yes, he is probably low risk, but I don't think we can afford any risk on this. We have to find him, kill him, and destroy the CD. He expects you to pay him because he asked for so little, so he won't be on his guard."

President Rock nodded and turned to Peter.

"Find him and kill him, but make it look like an accident and make sure that the CD is destroyed."

"We're on it, Mr. President."

Chapter 9

Peter and his men headed to their office and immediately began brainstorming over how to locate the blackmailer.

"This guy has to be an insider to have access to a presidential staffer, so we're looking for someone who works in the building and has access to the inside phone directory. He also has to know that Davis is a staffer. A secretary, maybe? Let's start with Davis' secretary and then everybody who knows that Davis is a staffer. Get moving."

Getting into personnel files and checking out the likelihood of all of those people being the blackmailer took several hours and yielded nothing. Peter and his crew were frustrated, so they sat down for more brainstorming.

"Think. Who else could have known about the meeting? Wait a minute, maybe I have the answer. Remember that before the meeting started there was a janitor who was in the recording area of the media room and saw the people who were present. He could have started recording the meeting before we got him out of there and picked up the recording later. He cleans a lot of offices, so he could know that Davis is a staffer."

"That's it! That has to be it. It fits everything we know about the blackmailer."

" Find out who he is and then check his phone records—cell, home, and everything else you can find. I want to know if he phoned Davis this morning."

A short time later, one of the men reported to Peter: "We've got him. We couldn't trace Davis' incoming calls because a staffer's incoming calls are untraceable, but we found the call to Davis on a cell registered to Robert Johnson, the guy who was scheduled to clean the

Media Room yesterday morning. I've got Johnson's address and his picture from his personnel file."

"Perfect, Gene. I want you to set up a remote trigger bomb in his home. Use something that nukes the whole place so badly that no one can tell whether it was a bomb. It should be so hot in there that nothing could survive and everything in the place melts from the heat. It should be so hot that it will be hard for the Fire Department to tell whether someone was there."

"I can do that. When do you want me to trigger it?"

"Give him ten minutes after he gets there and then light the place up. Since he obviously thinks the CD is the key to his future, he will have it with him. No one will ever find a trace of it or of him. Once you have the bomb planted, I want you to follow this Johnson from work to his home so that you can be certain he's in there before you detonate. Make sure this is quick, clean, and accurate. Get going!"

Peter headed to the president's office. There was no way he was going to report this on a phone line that may not be secure. Josephine showed him right in to see the president. He explained what his team had done and how they had caught Johnson as well as how they were going to deal with him. The president smiled. He was pleased and he told Peter so. He wanted a first-hand report from Gene as soon as the matter was concluded.

Getting in to Robert's apartment unnoticed in the middle of the day was easy for Gene. No one was around and unlocking the door was simple enough. His only concern was whether there was a dog or if a relative lived with Robert, but there was nothing and no one. The break-in couldn't have been easier. He planted the device where the explosion would rip through the apartment unimpeded by anything in its way. Gene was very good at explosives.

In a few minutes, Gene closed and locked the door and slipped out of the building. He left no trace of ever having been there. He headed back to the White House and quickly located Robert Johnson.

Gene kept Robert in view for the rest of the day at work and then followed him home. He watched Robert enter his apartment building. Gene checked his watch to begin counting the ten minutes until detonation.

Chapter 10

About an hour before Robert arrived home, Shirley Stevens climbed the stairs, pushed her key into the lock, turned it and opened the door. Shirley had decided to make dinner and surprise Robert. After all, she was his girl, she loved him, and she missed seeing him the night before. She knew that Robert had something important on his mind, but she had no idea what it could be. Could he have found another girlfriend? She doubted it, but she thought it would be best to hedge her bets and provide a very nice welcome home from work for him. A surprise dinner would work nicely.

When Robert opened the door to his apartment, he had no idea that Shirley was there until the smell of some of his favorite foods filled his nostrils. It had to be Shirley. Who else could it be?

"Is that you, Shirley? Something sure smells good."

"I've made some of your favorite things for you. I really missed you last night."

Robert walked into the kitchen and gave one of Shirley's large breasts a nice squeeze as he kissed her.

"You really know how to take care of me, sweetie, and I love your curves. By tomorrow I expect to have a big surprise for both of us. Get ready to go on some great trips because I am going to get some very serious money."

"Oh, Robert, honey, I know that you have big dreams, but where are you going to get big money by tomorrow?"

"Don't worry. Our fortune will be here."

Robert began tasting the food. "That's mighty good," he said.

"Keep your fingers out of my cooking, you bad boy. Now get cleaned up while I set the table"

Robert reached into his pocket for a cigarette.

"Oh no you don't! No smoking when I'm here. Smoking is outside only. Just go out and have one cigarette and the table will be set by the time you get back. Just limit yourself to one."

"Ok, ok, I'll go and I won't be long.

Robert headed down the back stairs to the little courtyard behind the building. When he reached the bottom of the stairs and exited the building through the back door, he stepped out into a sunshine-filled neat little courtyard. There were a few flowers, but the courtyard was mostly filled with neatly mowed grass, all of which gave it a pleasant smell. Robert put the cigarette into his mouth and lighted it with a match. He took a deep drag. How wonderful that first drag tasted mingled with the fragrance of the courtyard.

Outside in the car, Gene checked his watch. The ten minutes were almost up. He had no idea that Shirley was in the apartment and that Robert had left. He pushed the tiny remote detonator and watched for the result.

The blast was so sudden and so hot that Shirley nearly liquified. She literally was dead before she had time to realize that anything had happened. She only had time to hear the beginning of the blast before she was blown to bits. In an instant, the entire apartment was blazing. Nothing could have survived—no person, no animal, and no CD. From Gene's perspective, the job had been done exactly as ordered and would completely satisfy President Rock. He drove away to report to the president.

Out in the courtyard, the blast threw Robert violently to the ground. When he recovered his senses, blood streamed from his nose, ears, and mouth. He had cuts on his arms and his shirt was torn. He had fallen face down onto the ground. As he rolled over onto his back, he couldn't see the sky because it was covered with thick, black smoke. It took a few seconds for him to realize that where his apartment and Shirley had been a scant two minutes earlier, now there was only a large hole belching billows of black smoke. The apartment below it was also largely demolished.

As the fog cleared from Robert's brain, thoughts whizzed through it about what could have caused such an explosion. He had no gas appliances; everything was electric. So what could have blown up? At first, he had a sense of puzzlement. Slowly it dawned on him that Shirley was almost certainly dead and that maybe, just maybe, someone had tried to kill him. Why would anyone want to kill him? He couldn't imagine. Then suddenly he remembered about the CD and his request for money from the president. He touched his pocket and found that the CD was still there. He pulled it out and looked at it. It looked fine—not a scratch on it. It had apparently been protected from damage when he fell on his face.

Robert's brain continued to clear. Again, why would anyone want to kill him? He had shown his good faith by asking for only three million dollars from the president for the CD when he could have gotten a great deal more elsewhere. It was obvious that he was no threat to the president, and how had they, whoever "they" were, found him so quickly anyway. None of it made sense to him.

Robert thought that whoever was behind this, must have acted without the president's knowledge. His president could never do something so terrible. After all, this was out and out murder. He slowly got up from the ground. Although he felt a bit off balance, he seemed to be otherwise alright. He took out his handkerchief and wiped his ears, nose, mouth, and face. No one else was around.

Suddenly, panic set in. Whoever had done this, Robert had to get away before they discovered that he was still alive. Maybe it was an accident of some kind, but that was a chance he couldn't afford to take. He needed to find a safe place where he could think all of this through. But, where could he go?

Noticing that the courtyard gate had been sprung open by the blast, Robert headed for the gate. He raced through it and through the adjoining yard. When he reached the street, he looked cautiously in both directions and, seeing nothing suspicious, walked quickly across the street. He continued running through yards and checking streets before crossing for several blocks until he was certain that no one was following him. Only then did he stop to catch his breath and think about where he might safely go.

Robert made a sharp right turn, headed three blocks, then turned left for an additional six blocks, which put him almost at the front door of Dr. John Eber, his minister. Dr. Eber headed the Emmanuel Black Episcopal Church. Although Robert was a member, he only attended at Christmas when everything in the church looked beautiful and festive. Still, he knew the minister and felt certain that Dr. Eber could be trusted.

The street appeared clear, so Robert walked slowly into the doorway so as not to attract attention. He rang the bell. When Dr. Eber opened the door, he was surprised to see Robert, especially in Robert's disheveled state.

"My gosh, Robert, what happened to you? You are bleeding and you look as if you have been running. Well, come in and tell me about it."

"There was an explosion in my apartment and I think my girlfriend, Shirley, is dead. Since I can't think of anything in the apartment that could have exploded, I have to consider foul play, so you have to promise me that you won't tell anyone that I am here or that I've been here after I leave. Can I stay here for a day or two, at least until I have some idea of what is going on?"

"Of course you can stay here and of course I won't even tell anyone that I've seen or heard from you. I'm not married, so no one else is here. Now what is this all about and why would anyone want to kill you?"

"I don't know why anyone would want to kill me. Maybe I'm just paranoid or maybe something blew up in the apartment of one of my neighbors. I just don't want to take any chances."

"Alright, Robert, let's get you cleaned up. I'm just making dinner and you look like you could use a beer, so I'll have one ready for you when you've finished in the bathroom. I'll also turn on the news on

TV. Maybe there will be something about the explosion."

Robert thanked him and headed to the bathroom. He was astonished to see how badly he looked. Robert's hair was laying in most every direction, his face and arms had cuts, dried blood covered his face, ears, and arms, and his shirt was torn and had black soot marks. He was a mess. As he washed up, Dr. Eber knocked on the bathroom door. When Robert opened it, he was handed a clean shirt and pants. He tried them on and they fit reasonably well. After cleaning up and changing, he looked better and felt more relaxed. In his mind he began to question whether maybe he really was paranoid and maybe something in the apartment below his had blown. Still, it was best to be cautious for the time being. Better safe than sorry, he thought.

The food was really quite good, though not as good as Shirley's cooking. Thinking of Shirley brought tears to his eyes, which he quickly brushed away. After dinner and two beers, Robert and Dr. Eber relaxed in front of the TV. There was a brief story about the explosion, but not enough information for Robert to reach a conclusion as to what had caused it.

After a while, Robert started to nod off to sleep. It was early, but he had had a very trying day. He excused himself, headed to the bedroom, slid into bed, and fell into a fitful sleep.

Chapter 11

Immediately after Peter sent Gene on his mission to kill Robert Johnson, Rhonda Rock phoned and asked Peter to come to her office. When he arrived, she motioned for him to take a seat.

"After you and your people left us, I talked to the president about doing some further damage control in this matter. I think, and he agrees, that we need to find out what John Davis really knows and who he has told anything about this mess. Pick him up and interrogate him. He'll leave the office about 5:30PM and go out the main entrance. Intercept him before he gets to his car and take him to a secure place. And one thing more, let me know when you have him and where you will take him so that I can listen in. You also need to find out from him whether his secretary knows anything. Any questions?"

"No. Everything is clear. We'll handle it."

Around 5:30PM, John Davis locked his office and walked toward the front door. His secretary, Carol Norman, had left about a half hour earlier. Davis left empty-handed since he was not allowed to remove anything pertaining to the oval office, due to security concerns.

On his way to the parking lot, Davis was stopped by two well-dressed men. Peter showed Davis a CIA identity card.

"Mr. John Davis?"

"Yes, I'm John Davis."

"We need to talk to you privately about a matter of national security. Please come with us."

"Are you aware that I am a staffer for President Rock?"

"Yes sir, we know that."

"I have a dinner date with an old friend at 7:00, so will this take long?"

"It won't take long. You will have no trouble being on time for your dinner, and we will drive you back to the parking lot so that you can pick up your car in plenty of time for dinner."

Davis felt uneasy about going with the men. Why couldn't they question him in his secure office, and what kind of national security issue could they think he would have knowledge of? Maybe it had to do with that three million dollar phone request for the president Davis had received. Anyway, the men's credentials appeared in order, so he had little choice but to go with them.

Davis got into the car. Peter drove and the other man sat in the back seat of the car with Davis.

The man in back said: "I'm sorry but I have to put a mask on you so that you cannot see where we are going. I will take it off when we get there.

"Is that really necessary?"

"I'm afraid so. This is a secret location and you know the old CIA joke that we can tell you what is going on but then we would have to kill you."

Peter interjected from the front seat: "He's really joking about killing, you know. That stuff is just for jokes and the press, but we do need to keep the location secret. So, we appreciate your cooperation."

Davis relaxed a bit as he allowed his face to be covered with the mask.

After what seemed like a long ride, the car stopped and Davis was escorted into a building, down a hall, and into a room. Then the mask was removed.

Davis had to let his eyes adjust to the dim light. He saw that he was in a large lightly furnished room. There were no windows. The walls were painted a bright white, making the dim lighting appear somewhat brighter than it really was. There were only two chairs in the middle of the room, separated by a medium-sized table. Davis was told to sit in one chair and Peter sat in the other chair. The third man sat alone in a chair across the room. Davis noticed what appeared to be a small hallway in the far corner of the room, but he had no idea where it led.

At first the questions were quite innocuous. He was asked about his background, his family, and his habits. Did he smoke? Did he drink? How much and what? Did he ever take drugs? How much and what kinds? As the questions got more personal, he felt more and more uncomfortable. Finally, he objected.

"As a presidential staffer, I don't think you have a right to treat me this way. What the hell is all of this about?"

"All in good time, Mr. Davis, all in good time."

"That's enough of this. I am going to tell the president about this in the morning. I want to leave right now!"

Peter responded: "If that's what you want."

Davis got up to leave. He didn't even notice Peter giving a slight nod to the other man. Before Davis even realized it, the other man came up from behind and whipped a rope around him. Davis was rudely shoved back down onto his chair, and this time he was tied into place.

John Davis sat tightly bound in the chair for what seemed like hours. He would be bombarded with questions and then left alone for extended periods. He wondered: "What do they want? What do they really want?" He couldn't imagine the answer. He couldn't even be sure that these people were CIA. After awhile, all he knew was that he would do anything, tell them anything, to get out of there,

He thought to himself that he had been blindfolded until he was in the chair and that it was unlikely he would ever see the two men again, whoever they were. Everything seemed to indicate that he would be released when they were done with him. Otherwise why did they blindfold him? The car was a generic black car, he had not seen the license plate, and he was blindfolded almost as soon as he got into the car. The CIA credentials he had been shown to get him into the car were certainly phony and gave no clue as to the identity of these people. He knew next to nothing about them. Yes, he would almost certainly be released when they were through with him.

John Davis was reasonably sure that the interrogator believed that John did not know any of the details about what his anonymous caller had that he was asking three million dollars for. Davis explained that all he knew was that the caller asked for money in exchange for a recording disc about some meeting the president had had on Tuesday morning and that the caller said he would have asked for a lot more money if he had not been a strong supporter of the president.

Davis was also quite certain that the interrogator believed he had not discussed the phone call with his secretary or with anyone else. So, he reasoned, he should be released soon. Of course, he would report all of this to President Rock or to one of the president's senior staffers. Davis was correct that the interrogator believed him.

There was one thing, though, that really bothered Davis. Besides the other man, someone he could not see clearly sat in the far corner of the interrogation room. There was something vaguely familiar about the person, but he just couldn't place it.

The interrogator rose from his chair and walked over to the person in the corner. The two of them spoke in hushed tones for a few moments. Davis was surprised to see that the other person appeared to be a woman, but he could not quite make out her face.

He was startled to hear the woman say: "Kill him." Then she walked out through the door.

John Davis' face flushed. He strained at his bonds without success.

"No, you can't kill me! I told you everything I know. None of this could be of any value to anyone! Please help me, I'll do anything!"

The interrogator walked slowly toward Davis and sat down next to him. Davis noticed the syringe in his hand.

"Why?" he asked.

Peter quietly responded: "I'm sorry, but I don't know why. I am just following orders."

John felt the needle enter his arm and the sting from the liquid. His mind raced. Could this be a bad dream? Were they just trying to scare him into telling more? Could the injection simply be a truth serum? Yes, that must be it.

Then as Davis began to quickly feel groggy, the voice and the shape of the visitor came clearly into view in his mind's eye. His eyes briefly shot open in recognition of the person who had pronounced his death sentence. He gasped audibly: "My God, the first lady."

John Davis' eyes closed. His breathing stopped.

Chapter 12

The phone rang loudly, loudly enough to rudely awaken Sergeant Donald Hammond as he was dozing. He was supposed to be reading reports, but it had been a quiet night and the air conditioning system was on the fritz again, leaving the office rather warm.

He looked up at the wall clock and it read 12:47, which his slowly clearing brain recognized was the middle of the night. He hated the night shift. Even though he drew it twice a week, he never really got used to night work. "Oh shit, he thought, why can't people just let me sleep?" He picked up the telephone receiver.

"Homicide. Sergeant Hammond speaking."

"Sarge, this is Finerty. I know that you're probably napping and I hate to bother you, but this is important."

"Spare me the small talk, Finerty, and cut to the chase. Also, don't bother yourself about my sleeping habits."

"Ok, sarge, here's the skinny. We got a corpse down here, and it looks like he's a staffer for the president. I think you'd better take a look."

"A presidential staffer in your area? What in the hell would he be doing in a high crime area?"

"I don't know what he's doing here, but he sure as hell isn't going anywhere."

Hammond sighed. "All right, I'm on my way."

When Hammond arrived at the scene, he located officer Finerty. Finerty walked him over to the body, and Hammond began his examination. He looked at the location of the body, checked the body closely, and examined all pockets and personal effects.

"His wallet is intact and it contains $105, so I think we can rule out robbery. He could have been murdered, had a heart attack, or overdosed. I don't see any obvious tracks on his arms, so if he OD'd, he may have been a first time user and his body didn't like it. I guess it's a question for Doc now. Have you found anything else in the area?"

"We've covered the alley with a fine tooth comb and found nothing."

"His ID says his name is John Davis, and he has a White House Staffer card, so I guess we should contact White House Security. Do that and call the coroner's office for pickup."

Chapter 13

It was about 4:30AM when Robert Johnson awoke. He knew that he was in an unfamiliar bed, but he didn't immediately know why. Then it dawned on him and the whole explosion episode came pouring back into his brain. He shivered, and the shaking took a full three minutes to stop. He just lay there trying to comprehend all that had happened.

Robert got up and went into the bathroom. He looked better than he had when he first arrived at Dr. Ebel's house. He got dressed, but he didn't bother to shave. When he got to the kitchen, Robert found some bread along with a note from Dr. Ebel inviting him to help himself to anything he wanted if he got up early. The note contained an apology that there was nothing specially made for breakfast. Robert smiled.

The coffee pot was soon heating and Robert began making toast. He located butter and jam as well as a coffee cup, saucer, and a plate and utensils. He began to relax and think about yesterday's events. He thought:

"Maybe I was paranoid yesterday. After all, why would anyone want to kill me? It was probably an explosion in the apartment below. That place looked as blown out as my apartment did. Maybe it was even something in the floor. There must be lots of wires and pipes there. I guess I should phone the police and tell them that I am alright and describe what happened. Of course, if I do that they will want to know why I ran away. I sure can't tell them why because if I say that I was afraid someone was trying to kill me, they will want to know why and who. I guess I will have to think about what story to tell them. I also need to go to work, probably today. I can't just not show up if I want to keep my job. I also need to phone Shirley's parents, and what am I going to tell them?"

Robert concluded that he would have to give all of this more thought. There was no sense jumping to half-assed decisions.

By now it was almost 5:00AM and it was time for the 5 o'clock news on TV. He turned on the TV very quietly so as not to disturb Dr. Ebel's sleep. His timing was perfect. The news was just beginning.

"Good morning everyone. Happy Wednesday. It will be sunny and warm today, but more about that later when the weatherman comes on at ten after the hour. First the international news. The latest from Iran is surprising. The Ayatollah Koman released a statement to Iranian television that he considers recent overtures from President Rock will create a 'window of opportunity' to use diplomacy to resolve disagreements with the West. This is the first non-frosty statement about the West to come out of Iran in years. Don't get too excited about Iran yet, but maybe this statement is a start on the road to peace.

"The rest of the Middle East news is not as good. The Palestinians have fired rockets into Israel again, destroying a home, but no one was injured. The Israelis responded with an air strike that destroyed a house and killed three Hamas officers. Here is some video from the scene."

The video showed the smoking ruins of the Hamas house surrounded by crying Palestinians, many carrying placards scrawled with messages translated on the bottom of the screen as kill Israelis and Americans. As usual, there was no footage of the destruction in Israel that had caused the Israelis to launch their air strike. Robert, who did not like Israel or Jews in general, nevertheless wondered why he almost never saw pictures of Palestinian caused destruction in Israel on the news. He reasoned that the Palestinians must be favored by the Middle East news agencies. Oh well, he thought, that is their problem, not his. He had his own problems on this day.

"Here is a local story just coming in. Police have just discovered the body of John Davis, a junior staffer of President Rock."

Robert's mouth shot open in disbelief and his eyes became glued to the screen.

"Davis was found in an area frequented by known drug dealers. Preliminary reports are that he died of a drug overdose. He was estimated to have died sometime early last evening. Davis worked at the White House. Our sources tell us that he was unmarried. A White House representative says they will comment later when more facts are known, but the representative said that a loss of any staffer is a sad time for the president. Now let's get back to the international news."

Robert quickly switched off the TV. Davis was the staffer he had contacted to demand the money. Now Davis was dead and Robert's apartment had blown up. There could be no further doubt—someone was trying to kill him. He went directly into panic mode.

Chapter 14

Chaim Gol's mind wandered over a number of topics he was monitoring, but his mind kept coming back to the missing Middle East government representatives, his "targets." Why had at least some of them been in the United States at the same time, where had the rest of them been, and what the hell was going on?

His phone rang and when he answered he heard the voice of his assistant.

"All of the missing targets have returned and here is something very interesting."

"Yes, what is so interesting?"

"All of them arrived at their home airports from the United States, and all within a few hours of each other."

"Shit!"

"I don't like this, Chaim."

"Neither do I, dammit. What is going on here?"

Gol's secretary burst into his office with a copy of the Washington Post and pointed to stories on several pages. Gol excused himself from the phone call, promising to call back. He grabbed the paper.

"What's so important that you had to interrupt an important phone call?

"Take a look at the stories I have circled. I think that you will agree it was worth the interruption."

Gol began reading: "A really strange set of circumstances has arisen, at least two of which directly affect the White House, and a third one happened near the White House. All of them occurred within the past twenty-four hours. Late yesterday afternoon, an apartment house including the apartment of White House janitor Robert Johnson was heavily damaged by an explosion. Johnson is presumed dead since his car is still outside the building. Neighbors have told us that Johnson never goes anywhere without that car. Johnson was 36 years old and had worked at the White House for the past twelve years. So far, no one knows what caused the explosion and a Fire Department representative said that the damage is so extensive that it could take weeks to find the cause if it is ever determined.

"Incredibly, the same evening, the body of White House junior presidential staffer John Davis was found in an alley in a high crime area. It appears that Davis had overdosed on drugs, but a police spokesman said it may take several days before the cause of death can be confirmed by autopsy. Davis was 32 years old and reportedly unmarried. He had worked for the president for the past six years. President Rock's office has issued a statement saying that they knew of no prior drug history by Davis and that the president's thoughts are with his family at their time of sorrow."

There was more, but it added nothing of particular interest to Gol although it referred him to a related story about the death of a young boy on the same day. Gol turned to the related story.

"Rory Bean died on his twelfth birthday after falling off of a roof from a building facing the back of the White House. His new camera, his birthday present, was found at the edge of the roof where he fell. Police believe that he leaned too far over the roof and fell. Strangely, the camera was empty. The accident happened around 10:00AM yesterday. His parents are heartbroken. Besides saying that Rory was much too smart to lean too far over the roof, they declined comment."

The remainder of the story held no interest for Gol. He leaned back in his chair and tried to put the pieces together. Could two or all three of these stories be related? And, more importantly, could they have something to do with the missing diplomats? He had the uneasy feeling that something important was going on. He reached for the phone and phoned his assistant.

"Just one question: what time did the three targets we had under surveillance in Washington get back to the hotel?"

"They started arriving around 10:20AM and then they arrived at about five minute intervals."

"I thought so. Thanks for the information."

"Is something happening?"

"Yeah, I am pretty sure something big is going on, but I don't know what, at least not yet."

Chaim hung up the phone and directly phoned the Prime Minister. He was put through immediately.

"Mr. Prime Minister, I need to see you immediately and in person."

"Is this the same thing we recently talked about?"

"Yes."

"Come right over."

Gol immediately left his office for the meeting On the way out of the door, he told his secretary that she had done well to interrupt his phone call.

When he got to the Prime Minister's office, he was told to go in. He was motioned to sit down.

"Alright, Chaim, what is going on? I assume that you have something important that you didn't have when we last spoke."

Gol described what he had just read in the Washington Post and updated the Prime Minister as to the return of all of the missing targets around the same time and all from Washington.

"So, Chaim, what do think it means?"

"I don't have enough to go on, but if I were a betting man, which I am in this matter, I would say that all three of those deaths are related to our targets being in Washington at the same time. My educated guess is that there was some kind of meeting at the White House between our targets and someone high up in the government, maybe even the president. I think the dead people heard or saw something that they weren't supposed to hear or see and that they were murdered because of it. The problem is that this is all conjecture and I have no idea what could be so secret."

"Are you telling me that you believe someone high up in the White House is complicit in murder, including the murder of a young boy on his birthday?"

"That's exactly what I'm telling you."

"If you're right, it must be something really important."

"Exactly, and if it is really important and involves a lot of Middle Eastern high ranking people from countries unfriendly to Israel, then it's also really important, and probably crucial, to us."

"What do you suggest doing?"

"I don't know that there is anything we can do until we know more."

"I agree, so do your best to find out more. Keep me very closely posted on this."

"Right."

Chaim Gol left. The Prime Minister picked up the phone and dialed a number almost no one in the government knew about.

"Middle East Foods. Joel Drummond speaking."

"I have a food order that you need to know about, but it doesn't require any action yet. Stop at my office when you have a chance and I'll brief you on a new customer. There's no rush since the new customer doesn't need anything yet."

"I'll stop by in a little while. I can always use new business."

Chapter 15

Whenhen Rhonda Rock returned from the interrogation of John Davis, she reported to her husband.

"The Davis matter is finished. Peter will dispose of him in such a way that it will look as if he overdosed. I don't think he told anybody anything."

"Then why did you have him taken care of? He never could have identified anyone or the place."

"Just tidying up. He knew too much, so it was best to deal with him before he let something slip."

What about his secretary?"

"Yes, Carol Norman. Davis claimed that he told her nothing about the meeting and I am sure he told the truth. Peter knows how to get information."

"What do we know about her?"

"We have her personnel record. She is white, 5'3", 130 lbs., and never married. She is 36 years old. She was born in Madison, Wisconsin. Her parents are teachers. We know of nothing that would connect her to Robert Johnson, and she seems to have had only a professional relationship with Davis. She worked for him for two years. There is no reason to believe that she knows anything about the meeting or even that there was a meeting."

"Well, Rhonda, if we wanted to be totally safe, we could take her out, but I am concerned that we have two deaths the same day that are connected to the White House plus the kid's death next door to the White House. I don't think we can afford another White House death, especially the secretary of one of the people who just died, without having the local police, the FBI, and who knows who else investigating. You don't shit where you live. Unless we have something a lot more concrete against this Carol Norman, I think we need to leave her alone."

"I agree. She's home free for the time being."

There were two facts about Carol Norman the Rocks did not know that may have given them pause about the decision they had just reached. Although Carol practiced no religion, her mother, Edith Nelson, is Jewish. Her father has no religion. Her parents met in college and are now junior college history teachers in Madison, Wisconsin. The Rocks may have felt a little uncomfortable if they had known about her Jewish connection. They would have been bothered even more had they known that Carol was at least marginally friendly with Samuel Cohen, the Washington, D.C. Bureau Chief of the Jerusalem Post, a fact that was soon going become important to the Rocks. She had met Cohen on several occasions when he stopped by to clear the facts on stories with her boss.

In any event, the decision had been made. Carol Davis, though completely ignorant of the fact that she was in any danger, was safe for the moment.

Chapter 16

Robert Johnson knocked softly on Dr. Ebel's door.
"Yes, is that you Robert?"

"I'm sorry to wake you up this early, Dr. Ebel, but I need to talk to you about a really big problem I have."

"Alright. I'll get dressed and be right out."

Within a few minutes, Dr. Ebel emerged from his bedroom and greeted Robert. The two of them sat on the sofa. Robert brought two cups of coffee. Robert described what he had seen on the TV news about the death of John Davis, and explained that he had a recent involvement with Davis involving the situation that caused him to worry that someone was trying to kill him. Robert told him nothing about the president or the CD that was in his pocket.

"Under the circumstances, Dr. Ebel, I am really scared."

"Robert, I think you have reason to be scared. You need to go to the police immediately and tell them what is going on."

"I can't do that. I'm involved in something that could get me in real trouble with the law and the people I fear could control the police. No, I haven't killed anyone or robbed a bank or anything like that. The problem is that I know something that no one is supposed to know about powerful people."

"And you tried to get money from them in order to keep your mouth shut?"

"Exactly."

"Oh Robert, didn't you know what kind of people you were dealing with? Never mind, don't tell me anything. I don't even want to know who or what is involved. So you're in a real pickle. Now what are you going to do about it?"

"I think I should get out of here as fast as I can. They probably think

I'm dead, but someone may decide to make sure and one of the first places they would probably start is with my minister."

"Yes. I suppose that's right."

"I know of a place I could go where they wouldn't think to look for me, at least not for awhile. Could I borrow your car?"

"Of course."

"I will leave it several blocks from where I am going and I will call you and let you know where it is. I wish I could just take a cab or a bus, but I don't want anyone to see me. I also think it will be safer for you if I leave it someplace that doesn't connect it with me."

"That's perfectly fine. Here are the keys. Yes, I know, I haven't seen or heard from you. Good luck, Robert, and may God protect you from harm."

Robert bolted out to the garage, opened the garage door, and got into the car. He turned the key in the ignition and the car started. It wasn't as luxurious as his red BMW, but right now it was a lot safer. He pulled out of the garage, closed the garage door with the remote, and headed down the street. Several miles down the road, Robert parked the car, stopped at a pay phone, phoned Dr. Ebel to give him the car's location, thank him, and begin a long walk.

Carol Norman lived in a small house in a nice area. She was listed in the phone book, so Robert had no trouble finding her address. As he approached her house, he checked carefully for any sign of danger. There was none. It was 6:15AM. Robert pushed the door bell. No one answered, so he tried again. Finally Carol, fully dressed, opened the door.

"Robert. What in the world are you doing here?"

"I'm in a lot of trouble, and I didn't know where else to go."

"I guess you had better come in and tell me about it. Let's sit on the sofa. I have limited time because I need to go to work."

"I don't think you will be going to work today."

"What are you talking about? Of course I have to go to work. Mr. Davis has a busy day lined up."

"Mr. Davis was murdered last night and I think the same people are after me."

"What! Are you crazy?"

"Put on the news if you don't believe me."

"What is going on here, Robert?"

"I heard something that President Rock is planning. I won't tell you what it is or what proof I can lay my hands on, but it is very bad for Israel. I phoned your boss yesterday and had him get a message to the president that I wanted a small amount of money, well not that small but small for the value of what I offered. The next thing I knew, someone blew up my apartment and killed my girlfriend. They just missed getting me and they probably think I'm dead, but I'm afraid they'll figure out that I'm still alive."

"How can you be so sure that it wasn't an accident?"

At first I thought that was possible, but there was nothing in my place that could explode and I have no gas, only electric appliances. Then, the real thing that convinced me was when I saw on the 5AM news on TV that your boss' body was found this morning in a high crime area dead of a drug overdose."

"That's crazy. Mr. Davis was a straight arrow. He probably never tried drugs in his life."

"That's what I thought. It was murder, and right after my apartment exploded. Whoever it is wants everybody dead who knows about what I know. So, what do I do? I came to you because I'm friendly with you at work and my phone call to your boss is probably what got him killed."

Carol sat in stunned silence. This story was all too wild to be true, but why would someone make up a story like that? Slowly Carol turned to Robert.

"What do you know or have that's so important?"

"Right now I'm not telling anybody."

"Whatever it is, you think the President of the United States is trying to kill you to keep you quiet?"

"I think it is someone on the president's staff. I can't believe that a good man like President Rock would commit murder."

"You said your information has something to do with Israel?"

"It is all about Israel and it's very bad for the Israelis."

"Well, if you're right that someone in the administration tried to kill you and did kill my boss, then I'm in danger too.

"I hadn't thought about that, but I suppose that you're right. So, what do we both do?"

"I certainly can't go to work. I may never come back. We both have to get lost very quickly. Since this mess involves Israel, I think I know who can help us."

"I'm no Jew lover and I don't want to get involved with Israel. I'm not an anti-semite, but I just don't feel comfortable around Jews."

"Then I should tell you that I'm half Jewish, and you seem to get along with me pretty well. Anyway, we have no choice. We need help and we need it quickly."

Robert said nothing. Carol grabbed the phone book and looked up the address of Sam Cohen. She didn't want to phone him in case her phone line was tapped.

"Robert, we're going to the home of Sam Cohen, the Washington Bureau Chief of the Jerusalem Post newspaper. Since this concerns Israel, maybe he can help us. I know he is connected with the right people to at least put us in contact with someone who can help us."

"If you think I am going to give him a story for his paper that will hurt President Rock, forget about it."

"What you tell him is up to you. He's a good person and I think he will help us whether you give him a story or not. Let's go now. We want to get to his house before he leaves for work."

They left the house, turned on the house alarm, got into the car and drove toward Sam Cohen's house. Carol constantly checked for a tail, but found none. Everything was clear so far.

Chapter 17

Carol stopped the car in front of Sam Cohen's house. They were in a beautiful area and Carol couldn't help but notice that his house was so much bigger than her house. Being a bureau chief undoubtedly paid much more than a White House junior secretary. She walked up to the front door with Robert in tow. It was obvious that Robert didn't want to be there. Still, as she had pointed out to him, he had little choice in the matter. He decided, though, that the Jews would get far less than the whole story from him. He would tell them only enough to show them that he really needed help. He would do nothing to hurt President Rock, at least until he was certain that the president was behind the killings.

Carol rang the door bell. Sam Cohen appeared surprised to see Carol and a man he had never seen before at his front door so early in the morning.

"Come in, Carol. I don't suppose this is a social call. I just saw the story about your boss on the news. I had no idea he had a drug problem."

"He didn't. This is Robert Johnson, a sanitary engineer at the White House. We have quite a story to tell you, but Robert insists that you first agree not to print it."

"I promise that I won't print anything you tell me, Robert, unless I also get it from some other source. That's the best I can do. Fair enough?"

"I guess that's fair."

Samuel Cohen, known to most people as simply Sam, was 62 years old and married. He stood 5'10" tall at a fairly solid 200 lbs. Sam was friendly, very smart, and well connected. He was adept at getting the news when others did not even know it existed. Thus, he had little trouble putting Carol at ease. Even Robert felt comfortable, and was sure that he could trust Cohen. Robert was surprised at the feeling. Well, he thought, maybe he could trust some Jews.

"Alright, what can I do for you?"

Robert began. He explained that he learned something about President Rock that was very bad for Israel, that he tried to get money to forget what he knew, and that he had made his request through Carol's boss. Within twenty-four hours after his money request, his apartment exploded and John Davis was dead.

"Wait a minute. Are you telling me that you are the Robert Johnson who was supposed to have been in that apartment explosion yesterday afternoon?"

"Yes."

"Continue the story. What is it you tried to sell these people?"

"I won't tell you that."

"Alright. So what else can you tell me?"

Carol said: "What he told you is all I know, but I can tell you that John Davis probably never took drugs in his life."

"I see. So I think what you're trying to tell me is that someone is trying to kill Robert and that if your boss was murdered, you may be next on the list."

"Exactly."

"Tell me, Robert, does anyone know that you're still alive?"

"Only my minister."

"Are you positive that you can trust him?"

"Absolutely."

"Does he know that you're here?"

"No one knows that we're here. My minister doesn't even know that I know Carol or that I went to her house."

"Excellent. Carol, is there any chance that you were followed here?"

"No. I kept checking all the way here and I saw nothing. Actually, some of the streets were empty, so I don't see how anyone could have followed us without being seen."

"Good. You seem to be safe for now. They, whoever they are, apparently think Robert is dead and they don't know where you are. If you don't show up for work today, Carol, they may get suspicious, but I think it's too risky for you to go to work. Both of you can stay here temporarily, but you need to disappear, probably permanently. It so happens that I know someone who can probably arrange your escape, but it may take him a day or two to get here. Just stay here for now while I make a phone call."

Cohen dialed the phone number for Middle East Foods in Jerusalem.

"Middle East Foods."

"Joel Drummond, please."

"Just a moment."

Joel Drummond was the president of Middle East Foods. He was also a very special, very secret assistant to the Prime Minister of Israel. Sam Cohen didn't know that, but he had known Drummond for years and thought he was much too sharp and well-connected to be just a food salesman. Sam had never asked any questions.

"Joel Drummond speaking. How can I help you?"

"Joel, this Sam Cohen in Washington."

"Hi, Sam. I take it that this is not a social call, so what's up?"

"You're right, it's no social call. Have you ever heard of Robert Johnson?"

"I don't think so. Who is he?"

"According to today's news stories, he was killed in an apartment explosion yesterday."

Drummond's attention became sharply focused. This was one the three dead people the Prime Minister had just told him may be connected to some kind of meeting of Middle East bigwigs in Washington.

"Oh yes, I think I saw something about it in the news. What about him?"

"He's alive and well and sitting in my livingroom with the secretary of John Davis, another recent corpse. The two of them believe that someone connected to the president of the United States is trying to kill Johnson and the girl fears she may be next. I think they may be right. They need to disappear, probably permanently. I know that you have great connections, so maybe you can help."

"Maybe I can. It just so happens that I am flying to Washington later today, so I should be able to get to your place tomorrow afternoon. Then I can talk to them and see what I can do. In the meantime, I suggest that you keep them out of sight. If they brought a car, dispose of it. Have someone park it far from you. Can you put them up overnight until I get there?"

"Can do."

"Don't tell them anything about me yet. Just tell them that someone will try to help them."

"Ok. I'll keep them here and see you tomorrow."

Sam Cohen hung up the phone and returned to the living room. He told Carol and Robert that they were to remain in his house at all times. No one was to see them or know that they were there. He also told them that by late tomorrow they would meet with someone who could probably help them. He told them nothing about Drummond. He introduced his wife and told her to get them whatever they needed and to tell no one they were there.

Next, he phoned his office and assigned one of his staff to come to his house and move Carol's car to the parking lot at the main bus station. The staff member could then take a local subway to the office. He was instructed to tell no one about this assignment and to ask no questions.

In Israel, Joel Drummond picked up the phone and dialed the Prime Minister's private number. The Prime Minister answered.

"Mr. Prime Minister, this is Joel. Can you get me on today's flight to Washington? It's really important."

"Of course. They always hold an emergency seat for us. You'll have to run. You don't have much time to make it."

"I'll make it. Do you remember the discussion we just had about three murders in Washington?"

"Yes. What about it?"

"You will never guess who I am going to meet with tomorrow."

Chapter 18

Ronnie Braun was the employee who received Cohen's phone call to move Carol's car. He was an old hand at this, so he knew the drill.

Ronnie walked over to the nearest subway station and boarded the train. He knew how to get to Cohen's house. He changed trains once and walked several blocks from the last stop.

When he arrived at the house, he rang the doorbell. Mrs. Cohen handed him an envelope with the key inside. The key had been carefully handled with a towel so that only Carol's fingerprints were on it. Carol had already wiped out the passenger side of the car, thereby removing Robert's fingerprints, and then placed her prints on that side of the car and the passenger door inside and out. If anyone found the car and tested it for fingerprints, they would find only Carol's. There was no longer any trace that Robert had ever been in the car. There were probably some of Robert's prints in Carol's house, but there was no practical way to eradicate them without being seen.

Ronnie took a pair of gloves from his pocket and put them on. Then he opened the envelope and removed the key. He opened the car door and got in. After starting the car, he drove it slowly and carefully to the main bus station in order to avoid a traffic ticket or accident. The main bus station was a large building and had plenty of parking spaces. Ronnie selected a space around the middle of the parking area, so that the car did not stand out, and parked it. He then removed the key from the ignition, got out of the car, and locked it.

Having left the garage and returned to the office, Ronnie placed the key in the envelope and placed the envelope and the gloves into his pocket. When he arrived at the office, he left the envelope in Cohen's in-box on his desk.

Chapter 19

After Joel Drummond finished briefing the Prime Minister, a phone call from the Prime Minister's office resulted in a seat on the next flight to Washington, D.C. being confirmed for Joel. He went home, quickly packed, and raced to the airport. He arrived just as the plane's doors were about to close for departure.

"Mr. Drummond, we are so glad that you made it. We were worried about you. Since you are listed as a VIP, you have been upgraded to first class and assigned a seat which has an empty seat along side it for your comfort. We hope that you will enjoy the flight."

Joel thanked the gate agent and boarded. He only had a carry-on, which he placed in the overhead bin. Then he settled into his seat. Within a short time, the pre-flight announcements began and the plane commenced taxiing. Take-off and the flight were smooth, and Joel dozed at times. Landing was a few minutes ahead of schedule, and he cleared customs quickly.

Louis and Clare Dror were Chicago natives. They lived in the West Rogers Park area of Chicago's north side and had attended Sullivan High School together. They began dating as seniors in high school and were married after graduation. Their wedding was at the purple Hyatt Hotel on Touhy, a place made famous many years later when a gangster was murdered in the parking lot. When the Drors were married there, it was a popular north side wedding site.

Soon after they were married, Louis and Clare decided to move to Israel. They packed and left their families and friends in Chicago. It took a bit of time to become acclimated to the new way of life and to learn the language, but they felt at home almost immediately. Louis began an international food brokerage business and used the name

Drummond instead of Dror to avoid the anti-Jewish sentiment in selling in some countries. The business was called Middle East Foods to avoid using an Israeli name for the same reason. Their only son, Joel, was born a few years later.

Joel was very bright and he got along well with almost everyone from the time he was born. He was a natural diplomat and could, as the saying goes, sell ice cubes to polar bears. He served his Israeli military time and stayed on for an extended term as a major on staff where he caught the attention of higher-ups. Thus, when the present Prime Minister came into office, he asked Joel to become a secret, special assistant doing whatever the Prime Minister needed to be unofficially done. By then, Joel was running Middle East Foods and traveled the world on business, so handling covert special assignments for the government was easy.

Since Drummond was born in Israel to American parents, he naturally spoke fluent English and Hebrew. He was a quick learner and later added Arabic, French, German, and Russian, all of which made him even more valuable to the government. He was handsome, and a muscular 5'11" at 190 lbs. He was 41 years old and never had been married, though he had had plenty of girlfriends. He simply never found the time to be married since he enjoyed his life as it was. Joel was so good at running the business that Louis retired and turned everything over to his son. Louis and Clare knew that Joel had some powerful friends, but they knew nothing of his clandestine government work.

After clearing customs in Washington, Joel picked up a rental car at the airport and headed to the Israeli Embassy, where he met with George Boles, chief of security at the embassy. Boles knew that Drummond was a "somebody," but that was all he knew. He had strict instructions from the highest level of the Israel government to give "Mr. Drummond" anything he wanted at any time, no questions asked.

Joel always stored a "black bag" in a secure area of the embassy that he could access anytime he was in town. Only he had access to it and even Boles had no idea of what was in it. When he picked it up, Joel checked to make sure that it contained his untraceable cell phone, a 45 pistol, lots of ammunition, very sensitive listening and recording devices, tracking devices, and an additional throw-away phone that could be traced. He told Boles simply that he was in on business and that he may need to reach Boles instantly at any time. Boles provided every contact phone number he had.

Black bag in hand, Joel got into his rental car and began his trip to Sam Cohen's house. He phoned Cohen from the car and told Cohen that he was on his way to the house. Everything was now ready for the meeting with Robert Johnson and Carol Norman.

Chapter 20

Robert and Carol spent Wednesday night at Cohen's house. Following Drummond's orders, they were instructed to stay in the house and away from windows at all times. They fully complied. All they knew was that some unnamed person was going to arrive sometime on Thursday who could probably help them. As she was instructed, Carol did not call in or go in to work on Thursday.

Claiming to give her condolences to Carol on the loss of her boss, the first lady showed up at Carol's office at 10:00AM on Thursday morning. Her real motive was to pump Carol as to what she might know about the Tuesday meeting. What she found, however, threw her into a rage. She discovered that no one had seen Carol since Tuesday and that she had not called in. She could understand Carol taking Wednesday off since her boss was found dead early Wednesday morning, but if she wasn't at work and still had not called in by Thursday morning, there had to be another reason. The first lady did not like the possibilities of what that reason might be. It certainly increased the chances that Carol knew something she should not know.

Rhonda Rock stormed into the president's office screaming.

"That bitch, Carol Norman, hasn't shown up or called in for the past two days."

"Is that Davis' secretary?"

"That's right. Now why do you think that little asshole is staying away?"

"Do you think she knows something? Couldn't she just be sick?"

"Without calling in?"

"I guess not."

"Listen, we need to find her and eliminate her."

"I don't like it, Rhonda. We already have two, and maybe three, deaths connected to the White House over the past two days. Another one, particularly the secretary of one of the dead people, could create a lot of heat on us."

"Not as much heat as if she knows something and tells."

"Maybe not, but if she knows something and stayed out of work because of it, she probably already told somebody. We can't kill everybody who might know something. Besides, she couldn't prove anything. The only person who had any proof was this Johnson and he's dead. Anyway, we have nothing connecting Carol to Johnson. We don't even know if they knew each other."

"You can believe whatever you want, but she works here, so she's an insider and people may believe her. I want her dead."

"Alright, alright, Rhonda. Talk to Peter, but tell him not to create any connection to the White House in this."

Satisfied, Rhonda Rock left the president's office and went to locate Peter. She quickly found him.

"Peter, you are to find, interrogate, and kill John Davis' secretary, Carol Norman. Make her body completely disappear as if she never existed. We want nothing to connect another body to the White House."

"The president has instructed me to leave her alone. Does he know about this?"

"Of course he knows about this! Are you questioning my authority?"

"No, ma'am. I'm just checking because I was told something else."

"Well now you have new orders. Any questions?"

"Only one: do you want to be present for this interrogation?"

"No. Just report back to me when you're done. Is that clear?"

"Yes ma'am, perfectly clear. My team and I will get on it immediately."

The first lady turned and walked out. When she got to her office, she was seething. She shouted to no one but herself: "Who the hell is that son-of-a-bitch to question my authority? I'll have him shoveling shit in the ladies' room! No, he may see some nice ass in there, he deserves the men's room!" It took several minutes for her to calm down. She was not used to anyone questioning her authority and she did not like insubordination.

Peter personally showed up at Carol's front door and rang the bell. There was no answer. He looked through the house windows. The house was dark and empty. He looked through the garage windows and found the car was gone. He didn't like the looks of things because it appeared that Carol had flown the nest. That was bad because he now had to find her or else the first lady would be all over him.

It was time to call in the rest of his team. One of them was to canvass the neighborhood to find out when she was last seen and where she might have gone. He was to impersonate a Fed-Ex delivery man and tell neighbors that he had a package that could only be delivered to Carol. He wanted to know where she might be or when she would be back. That approach yielded nothing since no one had seen her since Tuesday, no one noticed anyone visiting her, and no one knew any of her friends.

Another member of the team flew to Madison, Wisconsin, to find out whether Carol went to visit her parents. Even her parents did not know where she was and they claimed they had not heard from her recently. A check of their phone records showed that Carol had not phoned her parents. None of the neighbors saw any visitors to her parents' house recently. A check of local hotels turned up nothing.

Carol's phone records, even her cell phone, were also checked and turned up nothing.

Carol Norman had simply disappeared.

Chapter 21

It was late in the afternoon on Thursday when Joel Drummond arrived at Cohen's house. Joel wanted to cover a few preliminaries with Cohen before meeting with Robert and Carol.

"Sam, how are your guests doing?"

"Fine, but they seem to be getting a little edgy already. They are not the most patient people."

"What do they know about me?"

"Only that you are well connected and that you may be able to protect them. They don't even know your name."

"Perfect. Introduce me as Simon True. Do not tell them anything else about me or how you know me. I don't want them to know that I have anything to do with Israel."

"Right. Would you like to meet to meet them now?"

"Yes. I'll meet them briefly together and then separately, with Johnson first. I think he will have the most important story. You can be there for the brief introduction, but not for the individual meetings in case there's something they don't want to say in front of a newspaper man."

" Good. Let's go into the living room and I'll introduce them. You can use my den for the individual meetings."

They walked into the living room where Robert and Carol were anxiously waiting. Joel was instantly attracted to Carol. Sam Cohen introduced Drummond.

"This is Robert Johnson and Carol Norman and this is the man I believe may be able to help you, Simon True. The floor is yours, Simon."

"Hello. I want to hear each of your stories separately. It is very important that I know everything there is to know so that I can determine whether or not I can help you and, if so, how. In case there is anything you would rather not say in front of a journalist, Sam will not attend any of the individual meetings. His only role was to help you temporarily disappear until I was able to get here. Unless anyone has any questions, I will meet first with Robert in the den."

There were no immediate questions, so Drummond, now known as Simon, and Robert went to the den and sat down facing each other. Robert wanted to know whether Simon was a newsman.

"No, Robert, I am not involved in any of the media. I'm neither a newspaper reporter nor involved in radio, TV, magazines or the internet. The business that I run has nothing to do with the media, but I will not discuss my business because you don't need to know about it. That is my personal business and I intend to keep it that way. All you need to know is whether or not I can help you and that nothing you tell me will be repeated to any media person without your approval. Is that acceptable to you?"

"If I want your help, I guess I have no choice."

"Exactly. You may not ask me anything."

"Ok."

"I want you to tell me everything about this trouble you are in. Include every detail. If you're not sure whether something is important, include it and I'll decide whether it's important. Do you have any questions?"

"No questions."

"Excellent. Begin."

"I am a sanitary engineer at the White House. On Tuesday morning, information came into my possession proving that President Rock intends to hurt Israel if he is re-elected. I will not tell you what I found out or how I found it."

"Do you actually have proof of this that can't be disputed?"

"Yes, but I don't want to tell anyone what the proof is because I like the president and I want him to be re-elected. Besides, I don't particularly care about Jews or Israel. I could do without both of them."

Joel wondered what Johnson would do if he knew that he was telling this to a representative of the Israeli government. He simply said: "Alright. Continue."

"I thought that even though I support the president's re-election, I should get some reward for turning the material I have over to him, so I asked for three million dollars and pointed out that I could get a lot more from other sources and that I was doing the president a favor. In order to make this request for a reward, I phoned Carol's boss, John Davis, one of the president's staffers, and gave him proof of what I have. I told him I would phone him on Wednesday morning to find out if my terms were accepted. I did not give him my name or any way to contact me, and I did not tell Carol anything about this.

"I went to my apartment after work on Tuesday and my girlfriend, Shirley Stevens, was there already cooking dinner for me. I needed a cigarette so I went down the back stairs to the rear courtyard. Shirley didn't like smoke. About a minute after I got to the courtyard, the apartment exploded. I wasn't hurt badly, so I raced to the only person I could trust, my minister, who put me up overnight. I didn't know if someone was trying to kill me, but I don't think there was anything in the apartment building that could have exploded like that, so I just ran."

"I think you did the right thing. What happened to your girlfriend?"
"She must have been killed."
"Yes, Robert, if the police found any body parts, they probably reported it to the press as yours. It sounds as if whoever did this didn't know Shirley was in the apartment or that you had left it."

"As I said I cleaned myself up and slept at my minister's house. I told him very little about what I knew and I did not tell him where I went next. I woke up early Wednesday morning and turned on the TV. There was a story about John Davis, the same John Davis I had just dealt with, being found dead of a drug overdose. That sounded like murder coming so soon after my apartment exploded, so I borrowed my minister's car and went to Carol's house to find out what she knew.

I parked the car several blocks away and had my minister pick it up himself. I called him from a pay phone."

"That was very smart, Robert."

"Yeah, I watch a lot of crime shows on TV, so I learned something. Anyway, I told Carol about my apartment and about Davis' death and she thought that we should come here. She said Sam Cohen knows influential people who may be able to help us. She agreed that someone tried to kill me and might go after her next. I trust the president in spite of all that's happened. I think that someone working for him is behind this and he doesn't know about the killings"

"Why did you think to confide in Carol?"

"I am friendly with her at work. I stop by her office sometimes at lunch time, just to talk, and that's why I selected her boss to call with my message for the president. I like her and I thought I could trust her. I had never even met Davis. Do you think I got him killed?"

"I'm afraid so, Robert. If that's the whole story, send Carol in. The three of us will talk together when I finish with her."

Johnson got up and left. A minute or so later, Carol came in and sat down. Carol and Joel felt immediate electricity toward each other, but neither mentioned this connection.

"Well, Carol, I have Robert's part of the story and now I need your part in complete detail. I already told Robert that whatever you tell me will be treated as confidential. None of it will be released to the media without your approval. I do not work for any form of media. When you are ready, begin"

"As you probably know, I was John Davis' secretary. He was a junior staffer for President Rock until he turned up dead of what the press called a drug overdose, in a bad area of town. I am positive that Mr. Davis never took drugs and probably never set foot in that part of town. I believe that he was murdered, probably by the same people who blew up Robert's apartment. I have simply known Robert as a social friend—we would talk sometimes during our lunch hour. So far as I know, he never met Mr. Davis.

"I didn't even know that Mr. Davis was dead until Robert showed up at my house early yesterday morning and told me about that and about his apartment. I can hardly believe that all of this happened only yesterday. It seems like it was days ago. Anyway, I thought the two things were no coincidence and that I could be next on the list if someone killed my boss. When Robert told me that this whole thing is about Israel, it gave me the idea to ask Mr. Cohen for help. I know him because he would sometimes come to our office and talk to my boss to confirm the accuracy of a story. I figured if he is a bureau chief for a big Israeli newspaper, he might be interested in protecting people who know something that could harm Israel. I also thought that he had a lot of connections that could be used to help us."

"Is there anything else I should know?"

"That's everything I can think of, Mr. True. Oh, there is one other thing you should be aware of although I doubt that it makes any difference. I don't practice any religion, but my mother is Jewish and I think of myself as being Jewish. I told Robert that after he told me his story and I'm not sure he would have come to me if he knew about my Jewish background."

"Yes, you may be right. Let's get Robert in here and we'll all talk together."

Drummond left Carol in her chair. He got up and came back with Robert. When they were all seated, Drummond began.

"I have listened to your stories with great interest. The bad news is that I believe you are both in grave danger. There is no doubt in my mind that someone is out to kill Robert and that Carol, you may be next on the killer's list. Once you made the demand for money, Robert, someone apparently decided that whatever you have is worth killing for. Actually, the killer doesn't seem to want whatever you have. Instead he just wants to make sure that it and everyone who may know about it is destroyed. Whatever you have, Robert, is a very hot item. The likelihood is that the president is involved in this somehow, but it could be a senior staffer. We don't know who Davis told about this, so we don't even know whether the president knows about it. On the other hand, it doesn't seem likely that a staffer is murdering people without the president's approval.

"Now for the good news. I believe that I can help you. Robert, I know you believe that the president is not behind this and you could be right, but I doubt it. Anyway, I have a plan to find out whether the president is involved. There will be some risk, maybe a large risk, to you, Robert, in carrying out my plan, but I think we need to know if the president has approved these murders. Are you willing to put your life on the line to find out?"

"I guess I have to. We do need to know who the enemy is, and I want to get the SOB who killed my girlfriend, Shirley. I really did love her, Mr. True."

"Both of you, call me Simon. Now, give me some quiet time to put together the pieces of my plan, and we'll carry it out tomorrow."

Chapter 22

Early the next morning, Drummond was on the phone with George Boles of the Israeli Embassy. He needed Boles to help with a security issue connected with the plan to find out who was behind the series of White House connected murders.

"George, this is Drummond. I need your help. This is top secret—need to know only. Someone I am working with, Robert Johnson, will need some cover at the shopping mall where you have an operation. I believe that your cover is called Cream Flowers."

"Yes, there is such a store in the mall. What can we do for Mr. Johnson?"

"Johnson will be on the run when he gets to the mall, and I don't know yet who he'll be running from. I will instruct Johnson to walk into Cream at a pace that is unlikely to attract any attention. He will give your clerk the code name "Drum" and your clerk will take him into the back of the store. When your people are satisfied that it is safe, Johnson is to sneak out the back door and get into the back of one of your delivery trucks that will be sitting there. Your driver will leave on a delivery run and make at least two stops before depositing Johnson at a location he will disclose to your delivery man. After that, your driver will complete his deliveries and then return to the store as if nothing had happened. So that your people can identify Johnson, he is about 5'8" tall, about 170 lbs, and in his mid-thirties, and he is black. He knows me as Simon True, and he knows nothing about my connection to Israel or even that I am Jewish. I don't want anything about Israel or Jews mentioned to him."

"I'll alert my people immediately."

"One more thing—if anyone ever asks, none of your people have ever seen or heard of Johnson."

"I've got it."

"Thanks for the assist."

Drummond hung up the phone and headed into Sam Cohen's den where Robert was already waiting. Robert was an early riser, as was Drummond. It was time to brief Johnson.

"Robert, as I promised you yesterday, we are going to find out whether or not the president is behind the killings and particularly whether he is trying to kill you. We are going to set a trap for the bad guys. This trap will put you in some danger. Are you ready to do it?"

"I'm ready."

"Alright, then, here is what we're going to do."

He handed Robert a cell phone.

"Any call made from this cell phone will be easily traceable. You will phone the president from this phone and demand payment, except you will double the amount to six million dollars because he killed your girlfriend. I believe you have an internal White House phone book with his direct line, right?"

"Yes."

"I will give you a script to read from. The president will be shocked to hear from you because everyone thinks that you're dead. You will tell him that you'll call back later with payment instructions, and then you will hang up. The script will make the call long enough to be traced.

"I will be sitting at a café across the street to see who, if anybody, comes after you. You will leave immediately and walk to a mall five blocks away. You will walk casually into the Cream Flowers store in the mall and say the word "Drum" to the clerk. The clerk will get you into the back of the store. If no one is following you, wait until the store is empty before going in. When the coast is clear, you will be taken out the back door and into the back of a flower delivery truck that will be sitting there. The driver will leave with you in the back and, after making at least two delivery stops, he will let you out at a place that you will select about four blocks away from here.

"You will walk back here and come in through the back door. Do not enter this house unless there is no one around. You are to destroy the written script that I will give you if at any time you believe that you are being followed. If you are captured, which I doubt, you have never heard of Cohen, me, Carol, or Cream Flowers. Do you have any questions?"

"Will you meet me back here?"

"Yes, but probably not immediately. If anyone shows up after your phone call, I will follow them and find out who they are. I like to know who the enemy is. I am also going to give you a beeper that will be set to vibrate. If I send a vibration to your beeper, then you are in danger so you need to move quickly, and I will give you something to help you disguise yourself if necessary. If you believe that you are in danger, you are to push the button and send a vibration to my beeper, and then you will move quickly to get out of harm's way. Do you have any other questions?"

"No."

"Then let's get started."

They got into Drummond's rental car and headed down the street. After a number of turns, they reached a corner where there were two outdoor cafes directly across the street from each other. They found a parking spot around the corner and waited a few minutes until the cafes began to get busy. Then Robert went to one of the cafes and sat down. He dialed the president's direct phone number.

"This is President Rock."

"This is Robert Johnson, Mr. President. Are you surprised to hear from me?"

Actually, President Rock was shocked, but he quickly gained some composure. He also pushed a button on his desk that activated a tracing device.

"Mr. Johnson, we all read in the newspaper and heard on TV that you are dead. How do I know that it's really you?"

"It's me alright."

"That's great. I know that you work in the White House, so come on over to my office and tell me what happened. I should be free in about half an hour."

"I don't think that would be a good idea for me. I still have the CD you want. I don't want to sell it to the press, but because you tried to kill me, the price has doubled to six million dollars.

"I don't know anything about anyone trying to kill you. Do you think that the President of the United States would try to murder a loyal employee of the White House? I hope you think more of me than that."

"Maybe you're right, but I can't take that chance. I will call you later with secure payment instructions."

Robert hung up the phone and left it on the table. He began walking slowly down the street. When he was a block away, he began to quicken his pace as he turned the corner and headed for the mall.

Chapter 23

Joel Drummond sat patiently at a café across the street from where Robert left the cell phone he had used to phone the president. Drummond was in a light disguise so that whoever showed up to try find Robert would never notice him again should they meet in the future. The disguise was simple—a light wig, glasses, and a small beard. Otherwise, Drummond was dressed in dress slacks and a short sleeve shirt.

Joel was always prepared for any contingency, but what happened about eight minutes after Robert left caught him unawares. He heard a flapping noise and looked up to see a helicopter hovering over the intersection where he was sitting, which was followed by a plain, dark car about a minute later. All he could think was: "Shit, they got here really fast, and they sent a helicopter to boot. They will be able to check the whole area in a few minutes. I'd better let Robert know that he is in danger."

Drummond pushed the button on his beeper. Robert felt the vibration of his beeper and immediately went in to a panic mode. He stepped into the first driveway he could find. Once there, he took off his jacket and reversed it so that it was now light grey. Then he put on a plain cap and quickly, but not quickly enough to call attention to himself, headed toward the mall.

At the café, the two men who had arrived in the dark car produced CIA credentials and immediately began to question the café patrons to try to get a description of what Robert was wearing. One of them remembered him and described him as having a green jacket and no hat. He pointed in the direction Robert had gone. Robert had taken the precaution of starting in a direction that did not directly lead to the mall, and then he began going toward the mall after he had turned the corner. Thus, the president's men were initially misdirected, but Drummond figured that the deception would buy only five minutes of time at most.

The helicopter continued to circle an area several blocks wide. When Robert heard the flapping sound coming toward him, he was astute enough to step into a doorway. He knew that would not hide him very long, so he then stepped out onto the sidewalk and began walking. The trick worked. The helicopter pilot noticed Robert, but he thought Robert had just come out of a store and, besides, his clothing did not match the clothing described by the café patron. He did not believe the target would walk right out in front of everyone rather than hide in a store. Drummond had told Robert that hiding in a store near the café was a prescription for getting caught since those stores would almost certainly be searched. Instead, he was told that the safest place was the Cream Flowers shop in the mall, so that's where he continued to go.

Now, the two men from the dark car began to rapidly check stores, first in one direction and then in another. Had there been more men, they might have caught Robert walking on the street, but two men were not enough to locate him since Robert had been well-counseled by Drummond. Of course, President Rock did not know that Robert had professional help, so he never considered the need for more personnel. Without Drummond's help, escape would have been unlikely.

Robert now continued at a brisk, but not overly fast, pace toward the mall, with his pursuers not far behind. Neither knew where the other was, but the pursuers had the advantage of the helicopter. Finally, Robert spotted the mall a scant block ahead and he began to feel a little more confident. Then the helicopter flew over him again and circled for a better look while he held his pace but did not look up.

The helicopter pilot thought it was strange that, while most people looked up, the man in the light grey jacket and cap did not. The pilot alerted the ground team of the suspicious behavior and he continued to keep Robert in sight. When Robert finally entered the mall, the helicopter pilot again alerted the ground team, which was made up of Peter and Gene, the president's usual dirty-work team. Peter received the communication, and he phoned Gene, who had gone in a different direction.

"Gene, the copter reported some suspicious behavior. There was a guy who never looked up when the copter got close, while most other people looked up Maybe that guy didn't want the pilot to see his face. He is wearing a grey jacket and a cap, which doesn't fit the description we got at the café, but I think it's worth a look. I'm going to follow him. I'll keep you posted. Have you found anything yet?"

"Absolutely nothing. Nobody has reported seeing this guy. Maybe he had a car."

"I doubt it. The copter probably would have spotted him, and the only suspicious activity reported by the pilot is the grey jacket guy. Even that may turn out to be nothing."

"Ok, Peter, I'll stay in touch. Why didn't the boss call in more help?"

"Probably because the fewer people who know about this, the better."

"I guess you're right. I'll check in later."

Just then, the helicopter pilot called Peter to tell him that the man in the grey jacket had just entered the mall. Peter picked up his pace. It would not be easy to find a single individual in that busy mall. He reached the mall and went through the doors only to find a mass of people. Thus far, there was no grey jacket and cap in sight. Suddenly, Peter saw a black man wearing a dark grey jacket, but no cap. The pilot had said the jacket was light grey, but his idea of light versus dark grey might not agree with Peter's idea. Peter grabbed the man from behind.

The man quickly wheeled around.

"Who the hell are you and what do you want?"

"I'm sorry, but from behind you looked like someone I know. I made a mistake and I apologize."

"Just watch who you're grabbing next time buddy. You can get killed doing that, man."

The man turned and walked away. Peter decided that he had better be more careful in the future, because if the man had attacked him, Peter might have killed him reflexively. That would have been very bad since he was supposed to be under cover. Peter now began moving through the mall as rapidly as the crowded conditions permitted. He decided to check inside of only those stores where a man could go without being noticed. There was insufficient time to go through every store in the mall.

In the meantime, Robert located Cream Flowers, but someone was looking at flowers there so he had to wait. Off came the hat and jacket, both of which were rolled into a tight ball and now were carried under Robert's arm. Robert was perspiring from the stress of waiting. Finally the customer left and the store was empty. Robert walked in and caught the attention of the clerk, a nice looking man in his mid-thirties.

"Can I help you, sir?"

"Drum."

The man looked through the store window, but saw nothing suspicious.

"You may be interested in something in the back. Move quickly please while no one is looking in here through the window."

Robert followed where the clerk pointed through the curtain. The clerk remained in the store to make sure that no one noticed what was going on in the store. A scant thirty seconds later, Peter glanced into Cream Flowers as he passed by. He had no interest in that store because any man going in there would be too easily noticed. Instead, Peter headed for the sporting goods stores, especially those with jackets that a man could change to if he did not want to be spotted. He thought he knew his man.

When Robert went into the back room, he saw loads of flowers of every kind and color. The smells all mingled together, and that, combined with the rainbow of colors, almost overwhelmed his senses. He said "wow" out loud before he could stop himself. It was so cold back there that he put his jacket back on and put the cap into the jacket pocket. He felt a soft tap on his shoulder and turned around. A man, not the clerk who had sent him back there, handed him a white jacket that had "Cream Flowers" emblazoned on it.

"Please put on the jacket over the one you are wearing. You are to leave nothing of yours here when you leave. I will check the rear and I'll let you know when it is safe to go to the truck. Just sit tight for now."

Peter finished his canvassing of the mall without success. He checked in with the pilot.

"I've lost him. Have you seen him leave?"

"No, but I can't watch every exit all the time, even from a helicopter. Do you want me to stay here for a while?"

"I guess not. I'll check in with Gene, so hang on until I get back to you."

"Gene, have you found anything?"

"Nothing. I think he got away."

"I agree. Nothing here either. Let's call the search off and meet back at the car. We'll go to the warehouse office to a secure phone and report in."

"The boss won't be happy."

"That's not the biggest problem. The biggest problem is his wife, but we'll just have to deal with her. I'll see you in a few minutes."

Peter instructed the helicopter pilot to return to base, and he began a slow walk back to the car parked outside of the café. He thought of what he might tell the president. Losing Johnson wasn't his fault, Peter reasoned. If the president wanted Johnson so badly, he should have put more people on the street, but he knew that he couldn't say that. He also knew that the bitch, the president's wife, would be ranting and raving at him the next time she saw him. As usual, he would take the blame for everything. It was always somebody else's fault. In that regard, the president and the first lady were like two peas in a pod.

The man in the back of the store motioned to Robert.

"There was a helicopter out there, but it has left and no one is around. Here, take these flowers, cover your face with them, and put them into the rear of the truck. Then you get in the back with the flowers and close the door from the inside but don't lock it because I am going to put more flowers in there before we leave. Don't get into the back unless you can do it with no one seeing you. If there is anyone out there, put the flowers into the back of the truck and come back in here."

No one was there to be seen and the helicopter was neither seen nor heard, so Robert picked up the flowers, went out the back door, opened the back of the truck, and placed the flowers in. Then, looking as if he was going to straighten out the flowers, Robert jumped into the back of the truck and closed the door. Nobody had seen him, and he breathed a sigh of relief.

After several minutes, the driver picked up more flowers and exited through the back door of the shop. He opened the back door of the truck and placed the flowers inside, saying nothing to Robert. He did that two more times. Then he closed the back door of the truck and locked it. He got in, started the engine, and drove away.

The driver began his deliveries. He stopped three times to deliver flowers. Each time, he said nothing to Robert. Then he stopped on a side street, got out, and opened the rear door. This time he spoke to Robert.

"Take off the Cream Flowers jacket and leave it in the back of the truck. Then take off your jacket and carry it. This is where I'm supposed to drop you off. Do you know where you are?"

"Yes. I can see some familiar landmarks."

He got out of the truck and thanked the driver. Wordlessly, the driver got back into the truck and drove away. Robert walked four blocks to Cohen's house. Since no one was outside, he walked around to the back of the house. He tapped lightly on the back door. Mrs. Cohen let him in.

Chapter 24

When Peter and Gene arrived at the café, Drummond did more than observe them. He appeared to be talking on his cell phone, but the phone incorporated a powerful color camera with zoom close-up capability. Drummond wanted to know who the enemy was and here was his opportunity. Thus, he shot a series of photos, long shots and close-ups, of Peter and Gene as he looked to be talking and drinking coffee.

Peter had parked his car at the curb by the café across the street from where Drummond was sitting. It was a no-parking zone, but the car was marked with a CIA emblem which allowed for parking anywhere. When Peter and Gene left the car to search for Robert Johnson, Drummond put his cell phone into his pocket and walked across the street. As he brushed past the CIA car, he deftly attached a magnetic homing device to it without even breaking stride. Now the hunters had unknowingly become the hunted.

Drummond went to his car around the corner, turned on the homing device receiver, and patiently waited for it to show that the CIA car was moving. After nearly an hour, Peter and Gene returned to their car, started the engine, and drove off. That was what Drummond had been waiting for. Now the second part of his plan was underway: determining who these people worked for. Was it the president or someone else and, if someone else, who? And, most important of all, who was ultimately calling the shots?

Joel Drummond started his car and began to follow the CIA car via the homing device. That permitted following from several blocks behind without being seen. After a lengthy drive with a number of turns, Drummond found himself in a commercial area. When the CIA car stopped, it was time to speed up in order to see where the two men went when they got out of their car. He was on them almost before he realized it. There were Peter and Gene leaving their car and beginning to walk across the street toward a building that looked from the outside like a warehouse, dark and squat. It was a building anyone could drive past many times without even noticing it. That would probably make it perfect, Drummond thought, for whatever nasty purposes the two men had in mind from time to time.

The men unlocked the warehouse door and walked inside. Drummond easily found a nearby parking space and parked. Next, he reached into his black bag and extracted a very sensitive listening device. He set it up and plugged it into a recording device that was activated by sound. He aimed it at the warehouse, hoping that there was no one other than the two men speaking inside. There was nothing to do now but wait.

As luck would have it, Peter and Gene were the only people in the building. Actually, few people knew of its existence as a government facility, and even fewer knew that it was the place where John Davis had been murdered. It contained something the two men wanted, a secure, untraceable phone from which calls could be made directly to the highest levels of the White House.

As Drummond listened, Peter dialed a phone number which Drummond's equipment showed was at the White House, but it was unable to show who was the recipient of the call. Drummond knew that meant the two men were phoning a very high ranking government official. Unfortunately, his equipment could not hear what the recipient of the call said, so, hopefully, Peter would repeat a lot of the conversation to the other man present.

"Sir, this is Peter....Yes, this is a secure phone. I'm at the warehouse....Yes, sir, we used the helicopter and Gene checked out everything on foot. He gave us the slip. We traced Johnson to a café and got a description of what he was wearing from a patron, but we couldn't find anyone matching that clothing description. The copter pilot was suspicious of someone dressed differently because he never looked up at the copter. I followed him into a large mall, but I never found him and the pilot didn't see him leave. In the meantime, Gene checked stores in a different direction and found nothing. We got the cell phone. He left it on a table, so he must have left in a big hurry or was afraid we could trace it while he carried it. Maybe he heard the copter. We'll bring it in so it can be tested for fingerprints to confirm that the caller was really Johnson.

"Yes, sir, I understand. We'll do it, but we need some hard evidence about where each of them is, and right now we don't know where to look. Johnson's car, we understand that's his favorite possession, is still in front of his apartment, so we can't trace him that way. We've checked and he has not contacted his parents and we don't know who his friends are. I suppose that someone could be hiding him, or he could be dead and someone knows enough to try to get money from you."

Drummond's ears perked up with that last statement. It probably meant that the person on the other end of the conversation was either the president or someone who controlled the presidential re-election funds.

"Sir, we are checking everything.…Yes, we have checked out every conceivable place that she could have gone, and I mean every place. No luck. She has just disappeared without a trace.…No, we have not found her car and we have an all points bulletin on it.…Yes sir, we'll bring the cell phone right in for fingerprint analysis, and then we'll report directly to your office. Goodbye, sir."

There was a long silence during which only the men's breathing could be heard. Then Peter began to speak.

"Well, Gene, I spoke directly to President Rock. You heard me explain the problems, but he wasn't happy. When we get back, we'll drop off the cell phone for fingerprint testing and then we'll meet with the president and the first lady."

"Shit, that witch will crucify us for not finding the guy who phoned the president, whoever he was, not that she could do any better even with her big mouth."

Peter laughed.

"Alright , now watch your tongue, Gene. That's the first lady of the United States you're talking about."

"I know it, but she is a witch."

"You're right, but we're not supposed to say it. According to the president, the plan is this: find the caller and kill him. If we find who we think is the caller but we're not sure, interrogate him if possible and then kill him no matter who he is. No one we interrogate is to remain alive. Also, we are to find that Carol Norman, no matter where she is, interrogate her if possible, and kill her. We are to kill her immediately if we can't safely kidnap her for interrogation. Same deal for Johnson or whoever made that cell phone call."

"Well, Peter, killing is what we do best."

"That's right. Davis, the kid, probably Johnson. Yeah, we're good at it alright. Now let's get out of here and to the White House. We don't want to be accused of being too slow."

As they began to leave, Drummond quickly left his car, walked over to the CIA car and, after checking to see that no one was looking, he removed and pocketed the homing device. Then he entered his car and drove away before Peter and Gene left the warehouse. Since Peter had parked across the street from the building, the building's security cameras failed to record Drummond removing the homing device. The president's people still did not know that Drummond existed.

Joel Drummond drove directly to Cohen's house. Along the way, he constantly checked for anyone tailing him. He found no one. When he arrived, he parked around the corner. He walked around the house and knocked on the back door. Mrs. Cohen let him in. He went to the den where Robert and Carol were waiting for him.

Robert described his ordeal and how well his escape had gone after a close call. Drummond nodded his head affirmatively.

"We were pretty lucky, Robert. I didn't expect them to use a helicopter. I'll remember that for the future in dealing with these people. Did you leave your fingerprints on the phone so that they know you are still alive?"

"Yes, as you told me to."

"Excellent, I want them to be frightened and confused for now. Well, here is what we have all been waiting for. This may be unbelievable, but we have the information we want on a recording so we know that it's correct. Are you ready to hear it?"

They both said they were ready, but Drummond knew they were quite unprepared for what they were about to hear. It is not an easy thing to listen to someone talk about killing you, and that was exactly what Robert and Carol were about to hear. Drummond played the entire recording. At the conclusion of the recording, Robert and Carol stared in disbelief. Carol spoke first.

"My god, these people are monsters. You must have something really damning against the president, Robert."

"Yes, I do, but I'm still not talking about what it is. This is scary. I'm going to think about what to do."

Carol said: "Mr. True, can't you turn that recording over to the police, the FBI, the press or somebody who can do something about these people?"

"Unfortunately, nothing would probably be done and no news service would air or print it because this Peter only says he was speaking to the president. We don't have the president's voice on the recording telling anyone to kill anyone. So, we have only second-hand evidence of the president's involvement, and that's not good enough. In spite of the shortcomings of the recording, Robert do you have any more doubts about who is behind the killings?"

"No, I guess not. It's pretty clear, isn't it?"

"Quite clear, I would say. It is also very clear that the two of you are in extreme danger, as is anyone hiding you. Therefore, I have to get both of you out of here to places where no one would ever look for you. I've got some ideas about that, and I'm going to begin making the arrangements right now. I want both of you to stay completely out of sight. Don't even go near a window and don't answer the door for anyone."

Chapter 25

Peter dropped off the cell phone for fingerprint analysis and left word to phone the results to the president's office as soon as possible. Then he and Gene reported to the president's office. Only the president was there, and President Rock looked unhappy.

"What in the hell took you so long to get here?"

"Gene and I got here as fast as we could, but we needed to drop the cell phone off for analysis."

"Yes, of course that's right. How can a person avoid being caught by my two experts and a helicopter?"

"We don't know. We were there pretty quickly. We might have been more successful with more people on the ground."

"Maybe, but I don't want any more people to know about this. I relied on the two of you to get the job done and I even put a helicopter at your disposal, and the guy still got away. How could that happen?"

"We just don't know."

"Could this guy have had professional help?"

"If it was Johnson, we doubt it. Who could he know with enough smarts to put together an escape under these circumstances? He had nobody we know of. If someone else found out about whatever Johnson knew, he could have friends in high places, especially if he's connected with the Republican Party."

The phone rang and the president picked it up.

"President Rock."

"I'm sorry, sir, but I was told to call in a fingerprint analysis from a cell phone to your office."

"Yes, yes. What is the report."

"I pulled Robert Johnson's personnel file and compared the prints on the cell phone to his fingerprints. They match."

"Are you certain?"

"Absolutely."

"Thank you."

President Rock hung the phone up. He took a deep breath and turned to Gene.

"Those were Johnson's fingerprints on the cell phone, so he's still alive. It seems that you can't even kill a guy in his own apartment. I'm not very impressed.

"I can't understand it, sir. I saw him go in and I detonated ten minutes later as I was instructed. No one came out of there alive."

"Apparently you're wrong, Gene. Either he got out alive or his ghost used that cell phone, and I don't think ghosts leave fingerprints, do you?"

Gene could only stare back. There was nothing more to say.

Chapter 26

Joel Drummond walked into one of Sam Cohen's bedrooms for privacy and took out his untraceable cell phone. He began to dial. The phone rang in Richmond, Virginia.

"Rabbi BenAmi speaking."

"Rabbi, this is Joel Drummond."

"Is there something I can do for you, Mr. Drummond?"

"I have someone who is in great danger. I need to hide him in a place where no one would even think to look for him, and I think your house would be such a place. He is black and he doesn't like Jews. He does not know that I am Jewish or that I am connected with the State of Israel. He believes my name is Simon True, and he trusts me to help him. Very high ranking government agents are trying to kill him."

"Mr. Drummond, excuse me, Mr. True, what makes you think he'll be willing to stay with a Rabbi if he doesn't like Jews?"

"He really has no choice if he wants to survive, and I'm not going to tell him where I am taking him. He'll see for himself when he gets there. One more thing you should know is that he has something, I don't know what, that implicates President Rock in a plot that would be very bad for Israel. Rock's people have already killed three people who they thought may have known about this, so if they ever find out that you helped this person you could be in danger."

"Are you certain that the president is involved in this murder plot? Do you have proof of that?"

"Yes, but for reasons I would rather not explain now, I can't go to the police or the press with it."

"I'm not worried about the danger and I doubt that anyone could ever connect me with this person. I'll be happy to hide him for however long he's willing to stay."

"I should also tell you that his name is Robert Johnson."

"The Robert Johnson who was supposed to have been killed in an explosion at his Washington apartment a few days ago?"

"That's the one."

"And you're telling that it was the President of the United States who had the apartment blown up?"

"That's right."

"Well, well, this sounds interesting. Bring him over."

Joel hung up the phone and walked to the living room where he found Johnson sitting on a sofa.

"Robert, it's time to go to a much more secure location."

"Where are we going?"

"You'll see when we get there. Pack your bag."

Joel located Sam Cohen.

"Sam, I am going to take Robert to a new secure location that you don't need to know about. I'd like to get Carol out of here too. Can she stay for a day or two at your sister-in-law's house in Maryland?"

"Sure."

"Have Carol stay on the floor in the back of the car throughout the trip. Your sister-in-law should be told only that her name is Joan Dean and that you want her to be incommunicado while you investigate a story she's given you. Explain that no one is to ever know that she has been there and that I am the only one who can visit her. Even Robert is not to know where she is. Use my Simon True name for visiting rights. I'll get her out of there as quickly as I can. Have your wife take her, which I think is safer than if you take her."

"I'll see to it right now."

Sam briefed his wife and then Carol on the plan. Carol packed her things and prepared to go. She and Mrs. Cohen got into the car in the garage and Carol laid down on the floor . Mrs. Cohen covered her with a blanket. Mrs. Cohen opened the garage door, started the engine, and backed into the street. Then she started down the street and headed toward her sister's house.

When they arrived at her sister's house, Mrs. Cohen pulled into the driveway and told Carol to stay put. After the situation was explained to her sister, Mrs. Cohen pulled the car up near the back door and quickly ushered Carol into the house.

Chapter 27

As soon as Carol had left with Mrs. Cohen, Drummond pulled his car into the Cohen driveway as closely as possible to the back door. Then he rapidly moved Robert into the rear of the car, had him lay down, and covered him with a blanket. It was now time to go, so Drummond turned the key in the ignition and backed out of the driveway.

He took the beltway around Washington and then turned south on Interstate 95 for the drive of just over a hundred miles to Richmond, Virginia. He drove right around the speed limit so as not to attract attention. He passed Interstate 64 and stayed on Interstate 95 directly into town. Finally, he exited and drove for awhile until he got into a part of town that appeared a bit run down but neat. Joel kept driving until he saw a Jewish Synagogue. The sign read Ethiopian Hebrew Congregation. He pulled the car into the driveway that led into the rear parking lot. The only car in the lot belonged to the Rabbi.

Drummond pulled into one of the empty spots next to the door and parked the car. No one was around, so he led Robert through the door and into the building. They walked down a short narrow hallway and into an empty office. Robert looked around the office in disbelief. The walls were filled with Jewish memorabilia interspersed with photos of black and white men together, all of whom were wearing large unusual hats. He now focused on the old wooden desk which was piled high with papers and an Old Testament version of the bible. The only more or less open spot on the desk contained a pad of paper and a pen.

"Where in the hell are we," Robert demanded to know.

"We're in Richmond, Virginia."

"What are we doing in Richmond and what kind of place is this?"

"We are in a place where the people trying to kill you will never find you."

"This looks like some kind of Jew place."

"Yes, it's a Jewish Synagogue."

"I told you before that I don't trust Jews. I don't want to stay here."

"Robert, if you want my help, you will stay here until I can make other arrangements for you. If that is unacceptable, you're on your own. You choose. Besides, I think that you will trust the people you'll find here. You might even like them."

"I can guarantee you that I won't like them, but you don't leave me any choice so I guess I have to stay."

"You may be surprised. Anyway, sit down while I locate your host."

Drummond left the room. Robert continued to look around and seethed, but he knew that he was stuck. He was going to be there until Simon True got him out of there, and who knew how long that would be. Suddenly he heard voices coming his way, so he got up and turned around just as Drummond came into the room with another man. Robert was so stunned that his mouth fell open.

"Robert, I'd like you to meet Moshe BenAmi, Rabbi of the Ethiopian Hebrew Congregation, a congregation of black Jews. Rabbi BenAmi will be your host while you're here."

"Good day, Robert. I am Moshe BenAmi. You may call me Moshe or Rabbi, whichever you prefer. Most of my flock calls me Rabbi Moshe and you can do that if you like. Please sit down while I walk Mr. True to the door so that he can return to important business in Washington.

The Rabbi left with Drummond and Robert sat down. He thought that meeting a black Rabbi was one of the most astonishing things he had ever experienced, maybe on a par with the explosion at his apartment and finding out his president, a black president no less, was trying to kill him.

Rabbi BenAmi returned and sat down behind his desk, across from Robert. He was 53 years old and had slightly graying hair around the temples. He wore a large, well adorned hat that appeared to have come from Eastern Europe except that it contained many bright colors. He stood 6'2" tall and weighed 250 lbs. Robert found him rather imposing.

"Well, Robert, I understand that you have major problems and I am happy to help you. You can stay here until Mr. True finds a permanent solution for you."

"Do you think that he can find a permanent solution?"

"I know Mr. True fairly well, and if anyone can get you out of the bind you're in he can do it. He's very good at that sort of thing."

"How do you know him?"

"I just help him from time to time."

"But, why?"

"He has done some favors for me."

"You're black, and most blacks don't like Jews, so what are you doing as a black Rabbi?"

"Robert, that requires a long answer, but we have lots of time, so I'll tell you about it.

Let's start with my background. I grew up in Richmond. I became interested in religion when I was young and I always thought I would be a Minister since I was raised a Baptist. When I was old enough, I went to a Baptist seminary and studied to be a Minister, graduating at only 27 years old. I worked as an assistant Minister in a church in Richmond.

One day, I took the congregation to a joint prayer meeting at a Conservative Synagogue, and I enjoyed the meeting, the surroundings, and the people. Afterward, I phoned Rabbi Young, the chief Rabbi at the Synagogue, and told him I wanted to learn more about the Jewish religion. I had learned something about Judaism in divinity school, but I decided that I wanted to know more. After all, Christianity grew out of it and the first Christians were Jews. Remember that Jesus was a Jewish Rabbi. Rabbi Young was a nice young Rabbi, and he was happy to oblige. So, I studied with Rabbi Young on Thursday nights and attended Orthodox, Conservative, and Reform Jewish services for a year.

"I was hooked by Judaism, so I decided to become a Conservative Rabbi. I studied in Jerusalem and was ordained there. I spent a year as an assistant Rabbi in a white Baltimore Synagogue. I was well accepted and I enjoyed the experience. One day I heard about a group of black Jews in Richmond without a Synagogue or a Rabbi. This was a chance to return home to Richmond and to do something for the black community, so I took a chance and resigned from the Baltimore Synagogue and returned here.

"I began ministering to my new flock by conducting services in homes. Most of my people had come from Ethiopia, so I called our group an Ethiopian Synagogue. I wanted more for my parishioners than simply meeting in homes, so I worked hard to raise funds for a building. The money came from blacks, whites, Israel, and a Jewish foundation in Richmond. I received considerable help from Mr. True, but that's a story for another time. We finally had enough money to build a small Synagogue. When word spread about it in the black community, blacks came to services out of curiosity, and some converted and became Jews. When we reached three hundred families, we had to enlarge the facilities.

"I was born John Rogers Sanders, and I legally changed my name to Moshe BenAmi. I even met my wife here. Martha was a member, having come from a non-religious black family. She came to see our services and liked what she saw. She joined the synagogue, became a Jew, and got me in the bargain. We were married six months after she converted. It's really strange how a chance meeting with Rabbi Young led to my becoming a Rabbi, which in turn led to meeting my wife. I guess it was all fate. By the way, Martha is visiting her mother for the next week, so you may not get to meet her"

"What was it that got you so interested in being a Jew, Rabbi?"

"Perhaps that's an even longer story, Robert. I always had some questions in my mind about how Christianity had treated the Jews over the centuries. There were murders, pogroms, the spanish inquisition, and the nazis, to name only a few. I was bothered by the brutality of the genocide because Jesus was a Jewish Rabbi. It just didn't make sense to me. Maybe that's why I connected so easily to the Jewish services. I am sure that they are rather similar in some ways to the services Jesus must have conducted as a Rabbi. So that was most likely where my original interest in Jewish services began, and I was surprised that the more I observed the Jewish services, the more I liked about them and about the whole religion. It's a very humanistic religion, you know, and it's steeped in a fascinating history over thousands of years.

"Since you're a Christian, Robert, you should know something about the origins of your religion. Do you know very much about it?"

"Not very much. I'm embarrassed to say that I'm not very observant."

"Don't feel too bad because most people are like you are, so permit me to tell you a little about the early history of Christianity. Christianity actually began as a small sect within Judaism. It's earliest practitioners were a group of peasants in a corner of the Roman Empire who followed a Jewish teacher, Jesus, who was born into a Jewish home in the Roman Empire and who was executed by the Romans.

"Jesus is probably considered a Jewish apocalyptic prophet. He believed that the world was ruled by forces that God was going to overthrow and replace with a new kingdom ruled by His new Messiah. So, Jesus taught about the coming Kingdom of God and that people had to repent their sins as well as give up their wealth and live for others in order to be ready for this new order. Jesus believed that people must follow the Jewish law, the Torah, so as to love God above everything else and to love your neighbor as you love yourself. Jesus, as an apocalyptic Rabbi, believed that all of this had to be done immediately because the destruction of the old kingdom and the beginning of the new one were imminent.

"This was the teaching that got Jesus into trouble with the Romans and led to his execution. Pilot ordered Jesus crucified and that was carried out on Passover around 30 AD/CE. Though there were other apocalyptic teachers, to his followers Jesus was different because they argued that he had not only been right, but that he was proved right when God raised him from the dead. Jesus preached about the imminent resurrection of the dead at the end of the world, but his followers believed that Jesus was really the first to be raised from the dead, so the end had already begun.

"Christianity began as the Jewish religion Jesus preached, but, after his death, it morphed into a religion about Jesus. So, while Jesus talked about the future Kingdom of God ruled by the Messiah, his followers believed that Jesus, himself, was the Messiah. Much of this change in doctrine came about through Paul, originally a Jew named Saul. At first, Paul did not believe in Jesus as the Messiah, but he became a believer when he had a vision of the resurrection of Jesus. Because of this vision, Paul became a strong missionary who led the conversion of pagans and shaped the doctrine of the early Christian church. He pushed the notion that the death and resurrection of Jesus could bring salvation for the sins of the world. So it was Paul who moved Christianity from a sect within Judaism to a mainstream religion. Although Paul was Jewish, he concluded that salvation is available to both Jews and gentiles and that it comes from faith in Jesus whether or not one follows the Jewish laws.

"While Christianity came to regard Jesus as being against Judaism, nothing could be further from the truth. In fact Jesus came from a Jewish home, was a Jewish Rabbi, and only intended to be Jewish, although the Gospels relate that he did not keep kosher. His teachings to love one's neighbor and to love God above everything else came from the Jewish Scriptures. He kept the Sabbath and followed Jewish customs, and his arguments about how to interpret Jewish laws were with other Jews. His followers during his lifetime followed him as Jews.

"Even with that history, Christianity became an anti-Jewish religion, but all of the distrust happened after the death of Jesus. Perhaps Christianity's anti-Jewish bent began because early Christians believed that Jesus died and was elevated to heaven as the Messiah, while most Jews could not imagine that Jesus could be the Messiah. They expected an all-powerful Messiah, not someone the Romans could torture and kill as a common criminal. It was that major difference in belief that began the distrust between the two religions. Once the Christians came into power in the Roman Empire, and particularly after Constantine converted to Christianity, they had the clout to deal harshly with the Jews and they have done so over the centuries. There is much more history between the Christians and the Jews, but I think I've given you enough for now.

"Of course, that's just a brief outline, Robert, but I hope you found it interesting."

"Very much so."

"Since I converted to Judaism after being a Christian Minister and you wondered why I had done so, I'll tell you a little something about Judaism and about Israel. Judaism, as well as the other two great religions, traces its roots to Abraham.

"When he was young, Abraham reflected on how the earth could turn with no one to guide it. Though he had no teacher and he and his family were idolaters, he continued to think about how and why the physical world works. Around the time he was forty, he concluded that there must be one God who guides the earth and the planets, and that God created everything. For him, the whole world was in error in worshiping planets, stars, and idols. He began to argue with people and told them that only the real God should be served by them. Ultimately, he went from place to place convincing people that what he believed had to be correct.

As has Christianity, Judaism has changed much from its beginnings. Traditional Jews consider the details of Judaism to be related to God's revelation to Moses on Mt. Sinai, but today there are a number of different denominations within Judaism. There are more, but the primary ones are Orthodox, Conservative, and Reform. Even among these forms, the lines of distinction are sometimes blurred. For example, some Conservative Synagogues would not even consider having a woman Rabbi while others do have a woman on the pulpit. Reform Synagogues do have women as Rabbis, while Orthodox Synagogues do not. Still, the basic beliefs of Judaism are the basis for all of the differing forms of worship.

"Jews direct their prayers only to God. They do not pray to Jesus, Mary, Saints, or likenesses of any of them, only to God Himself. They believe that God gave the written Torah, the first five books of the Bible, as well as teachings contained in the Talmud and other writings, to Moses. They also believe that the Messiah will come. It is a simple and, as I said before, a humanistic religion, and one I can and do identify with. Again, this is a super simplified description of Judaism, but I have many books here on Judaism and you can read as much about it as you like while you are here. Unfortunately, you cannot attend services, because I am supposed to keep you completely out of sight. Although Jews make up a tiny percentage of the world and have been butchered through the centuries, their inventions, medical discoveries, and writings have changed the world. They are truly an incredible people.

"Here is a story not commonly known. If you look at a U.S. one dollar bill, look at the eagle on it holding an olive branch and arrows in its talons. Then look above the eagle and you'll see thirteen stars shaped into a Star of David. Haym Solomon, a wealthy Philadelphia Jew, personally gave twenty-five million dollars to save our Continental Army during the War of Independence with England. As a result, Solomon died a pauper. George Washington asked what Solomon wanted as a reward for his services, but Solomon said he only wanted something for his people. The result was that Star of David."

"That's an amazing story, but what's the big deal with Israel?"

"Jerusalem is the historical home of the Jews. More than two thousand years ago, the Romans destroyed the Second Temple, thus ending any central Jewish homeland until Israel came into existence on May 14, 1948. Until that time, and even today, Jewish prayers refer to 'next year in Jerusalem.' After the centuries of murder and discrimination, nothing is more important to Jews than to have a Jewish homeland with Jerusalem as its capital. Now that has come to pass, and it represents the religious home for all of the Jews of the world, no matter where they currently reside.

"Israel was created as an independent state as a result of a United Nations resolution in 1947 recommending the adoption and implementation of a United Nations plan to partition Palestine. While Israel was given only a small sliver of land, the Arab states surrounding Israel invaded it the day after its creation, but, against all odds, Israel defeated their well-armed enemies. Israel has been attacked by the Arabs several other times, but it has always prevailed. For many years after the creation of Israel, the Arabs controlled half of Jerusalem and refused to permit Jews from entering it. During the 1967 Six Day War, the Israelis were victorious in re-uniting both parts of Jerusalem, and for the first time in over two thousand years, the Temple Mount and the holy Western Wall, called by Jews the Wailing Wall, came under Jewish control. Unlike the Arabs, Israel allows everyone access to all of Jerusalem.

"Israel's largest city is Tel Aviv and while Jerusalem is considered by Israelis to be its capital, other pro-Palestinian countries refuse to recognize that. Shamefully, the United States refuses to recognize Jerusalem as the capital of Israel, so no one born in Jerusalem who later obtains a United States passport is permitted to list Israel as his country of birth. The passport shows Jerusalem as the place of birth."

"Isn't that like saying Washington, D.C. isn't our capital if Israel doesn't recognize it?"

"Yes, I guess that would be true in Israel."

"How can some other country tell you what your capital is?"

"Good question. The only answer I can give you is that it's all politics. Anyway, Israel took the barren land it was given and turned it into one of the most productive areas on earth.

They have tried to make peace with the Palestinians, but have had no luck. They offered the Palestinians almost everything when Clinton was our president, but Arafat, negotiating for the Palestinians, refused to even make a counter-offer because he wanted the unlimited right of all Palestinians who had allegedly previously lived on Israeli land to return to Israel. Of course, that would have given the Arabs control of Israel so that they could destroy it from within. Israel does have peace treaties with Egypt and Jordan, but those are only as good as the governments of those countries. In the meantime, the Palestinians keep sending rockets into Israel and, when Israel retaliates, the world newspapers and TV only show crying Palestinians.

"It sounds unfair."

"It is unfair, Robert. It's politics driven by Arab oil. What have black people said about this kind of thing? Here is one example Not too long ago when there was going to be an Israel apartheid conference at the University of Pennsylvania, a group of black students took out a full-page newspaper ad saying they were offended by the term 'apartheid' being applied to Israel. I am proud of those students for speaking up for what is right."

"Now I've got to go because it's time for me to lead services, so I'll show you to your room. I wish you could sit in, but you need to stay there with the door closed until I tell you that it's ok to come out. We'll have dinner later. You can take any books that interest you or else you can watch TV, but very softly."

Robert declined the books and headed off to watch TV, but when he got to his room, he sat for awhile and pondered this new information. Then he switched on the TV.

Chapter 28

A loud ringing awakened Peter from a light nap. He had had so little sleep lately on account of hunting for Robert Johnson and Carol Norman that he had nodded off in his chair. Peter quickly came into full consciousness and grabbed his cell phone.

"Hello. This is Peter."

"This is George, one of the operatives looking for that black guy. I think I have him spotted."

Peter's body shot to attention, and his mind became perfectly clear. A wonderful calmness swept over him and a smile crossed his lips.

"Are you sure?"

"It's either him or his brother. He's got the same build and features as the picture and description. What do you want me to do?"

After getting the location, Peter gave instructions. "Phone Gene because he is much closer to you than I am. When he gets there, point out the target and you stand down. I'm on my way and Gene and I will handle it from there." As far as Peter was concerned, killing Robert Johnson was a secret mission and the fewer people who knew about it, the better. George knew nothing about Peter's connection to the president and Peter intended to keep it that way.

"Will do, Peter."

George phoned Gene, gave him the information, and told him that Peter was on his way. Gene thanked him and immediately headed for the rendezvous.

"Whatever you do, George, don't lose him!"

When Gene arrived on the scene, he sent George on his way. Then he got a good close look at the target, but not so close as to call attention to himself. He and Peter were supposed to basically be invisible, just blend in, so, until this project for the president was concluded, anyone who paid attention to either of them would have to be eliminated. Gene was uncertain as to whether or not he should take any overt action against the target until Peter got there, but he was quite certain that the man was Johnson and his orders were to kill Johnson.

Gene surveyed his surroundings. The man was walking toward a large crowd where he could easily disappear, but there was an alley between the man and the crowd, so Gene made an instant decision. He moved quickly toward the man and shoved him into the alley. No one was in the alley and it wasn't particularly noticeable from the sidewalk. The man looked like Johnson, so Gene thought he had made the correct decision. The man turned to Gene with a startled expression on his face.

"What the hell is going on?"

"We've had a hard time finding you, Robert."

The man looked puzzled. "What are you talking about? My name is Morton."

"Sure it is, Morton. Did you think you could screw around with the president and get away with it? Do you think we're stupid?"

"I have no idea what you're talking about. The president of what? I'm just a plumber, man, so get out of my way before I call a cop."

Gene chuckled and pulled out a revolver with a silencer.

"I'm afraid that the game is over for you , Robert, oh excuse me, Morton.

"Wait a minute, man. I'm not this Robert whoever he is. I've got a wife and kids. Please don't kill me."

Gene quickly fired three times into the man's face, obliterating it. Death was instantaneous. Just then, Gene's cell phone went off. He answered it.

"Gene, where in the hell are you?"

"Peter, he was heading toward a large crowd where I could have lost him, so I shoved him into an alley and terminated him. Look down each alley until you'll find me You'd better bring the car because we need to get him out of here. The boss doesn't want any more bodies traced to his house."

Peter drove slowly until he spotted the correct alley. He turned the car into it. The two of them loaded the body into the car and cleaned up the blood spatters. They drove to a secluded area of a river and unloaded the body. Peter looked at the body for the first time.

"Jeez Gene, what did you do to his face?"

"I figured we would dump him in the river, but we could erase his fingerprints and I would make his face unrecognizable in case he floats up some day."

"Alright. Are you sure it was he?"

"It sure looked like it was he though he claimed to be a plumber named Morton. I wouldn't expect him to admit he's Johnson."

"No, I suppose not. Let's check his pockets. I hope he has that fucking CD on him so that we don't have to keep looking for it."

They searched the body completely, but all they could find was a wallet and some car keys. No CD. They opened the wallet and found about fifty dollars, some miscellaneous junk, and a driver's license. The picture on the license looked pretty much like Robert Johnson, though it was not a complete match. The name on the license screamed out at them: Morton Ovens.

"Oh, shit, Gene, you hit the wrong guy. The boss will go crazy and his wife will be even worse."

"He was getting away and he looked like Johnson. What was I supposed to do?"

"I know. I know. Well, let's erase his prints, put some weights on him, and get him into the river. I don't think we should tell the president about this. If George reports turning this guy over to us, we'll just say it wasn't him so we didn't approach him."

Yeah, I agree. Alright, let's dump Morton."

Chapter 29

On his arrival in Washington from Richmond, Joel Drummond made a very important stop at the Israeli Embassy where he again went directly to George Boles' office. Upon finding Boles, Joel asked for, and received, the use of a secure scrambled phone for a call to the Prime Minister in Israel. The Prime Minister answered within a few rings.

"Mr. Prime Minister, this is Joel Drummond calling you on a secure scrambled phone from the Israeli Embassy in Washington. I need to report to you on what has happened since my arrival here."

"Go ahead, Joel."

"I went to Sam Cohen's house and met Robert Johnson and, yes, Johnson's really alive. I also met Carol Norman, the secretary of the deceased John Davis. Johnson wasn't completely convinced that President Rock was trying to kill him, but I set a trap the result of which proved conclusively that Rock was behind the attack on Johnson's life."

"Could you prove it in court, Joel, if it ever came to that?"

"Probably not. I have Rock's men recorded saying it, but I don't have Rock's voice confirming it. I could only tape one side of the phone conversation, but the evidence was enough to convince Johnson and Norman. Incidentally, that Carol Norman is some good looking lady, and she's half Jewish, but she doesn't practice."

"Come on, Joel, you've never had time for any more than a date or two with the same woman, so I'll assume that this is another short term woman."

"Maybe not this time. We'll see. Anyway, the two of them are in extreme danger so I parked Norman at Sam's sister-in-law's house, and I'm going there to see her as soon as we finish this conversation. Johnson is another matter. He has something linking Rock to some kind of anti-Israeli thing, but I don't know what he's learned or what he's got. I haven't pushed him on it because I'm afraid we might lose him altogether. He doesn't know I'm Jewish or that I have anything to do with Israel because he neither likes nor trusts Jews."

"Well, Joel, that doesn't sound as if we'll ever find out from him what we need to know. What do you suggest?"

"I'm not so sure we won't eventually get something. I parked him with Rabbi BenAmi in Richmond. You should have seen his face when he saw a black Rabbi. It sounds weird, but it was the safest place I could put him, and, who knows, he might change his mind. Here's the bottom line: I need to get both of them out of the United States before Rock's people find them and kill them. I would like to move them to Israel permanently. I need your help to do it."

"Do you think that's necessary? Won't this whole murder thing go away pretty quickly?"

"I don't know what Johnson has, but three people have died and Middle East bigwigs have apparently made a special trip to Washington to meet at the White House, so it must be pretty important. No, I don't think it will go away any time soon."

"Do you think Johnson will agree to emigrate to Israel?"

"He won't want to, but he'll understand that if he doesn't do it he's as good as dead, so I think he'll do it."

"Alright Joel, what do you want me to do?"

"Can you get a special airplane to Washington with some kind of Israeli mission, so that it goes through the private airport here without customs and with clearance by only our security people?"

"Actually, you're in luck. We have an El-Al government charter that arrived in Washington today. It's a short term agricultural trade mission that will return here after two days of talks. Will that do?"

"That will do perfectly. I'll tell you what I need."

Joel briefed the Prime Minister on his plan. The two of them agreed to put the plan in motion immediately. Next, Joel gave George Boles a simple briefing with just enough information to accomplish what was needed to carry out the plan. With the plan now fully in place, Joel left the embassy and drove to his meeting with Carol Norman.

Chapter 30

Mrs. Cohen's sister opened the door. Joel identified himself and was admitted to the house. He mentally noted that the sisters did not look much alike, but his thoughts were really on seeing Carol again. Mrs. Cohen's sister said that she had to do some shopping for a few hours, and Joel explained that Carol would probably be gone by the time she returned. Carol was surprised and pleased to see Joel, whom she knew as Simon True.

"Simon, it's nice to see you again. Where have you been? What's happening?"

"I've been busy getting Robert situated, but it's best that you remain ignorant of his whereabouts for now. He's fine. As for what's been happening, quite a lot. Robert doesn't know yet, because I have just made the arrangements, that I'm about to move him permanently. You are going to the Israeli Embassy."

"The Israeli Embassy? Why there?"

"Because it's safe and I have some connections there. You will have a private room and only the head of security there will have contact with you. He only knows that no one else is to know you are there, only I can visit you, and he has been told that your name is Sara. You will live in his extra bedroom at the embassy, so he will take care of your necessities and you will have a private bathroom. Don't worry, he won't touch you. You will only stay there one night, and then you will be moving to a permanent location."

Where?"

"I probably shouldn't tell you yet, but it's Israel."

"What! Israel? What if I don't want to go?"

"You don't have to go, but then you'll be on your own. Believe me, you're a very hot commodity in this country and I've had to pull a lot of strings to arrange for your safety. Besides, you are Jewish, aren't you?"

"I'm only half Jewish, and I don't practice any religion, but since my mother is Jewish, technically I am Jewish according to Jewish law. Well, I always wanted to visit Israel, but I never thought about living there. I guess I should start studying Hebrew. Is Robert going there too?"

"For now, don't concern yourself with where Robert is going. I haven't talked to him yet about the subject. Right now, he's safe. As for you, you cannot tell anybody, and I mean anybody, that you are going to the Israeli Embassy and then to Israel. Even Sam Cohen knows nothing about these plans. He'll only know that you're gone."

"Will I see you in Israel?"

"Carol, I'm trying to save your life so for now we can only take things one day at a time. You are seeing me here and now and that will just have to do."

"Simon, if that's your real name, I don't know who you are, but I can tell from the way you look at me that you have some feelings for me. I could see it, I could even feel it, from the first time we met. I think you know I have the same feelings for you, so it's only fair for you to tell me if I'll ever see you again after I go to Israel."

"I'm sure that you will. Yes I have strong feelings for you and since I have good enough connections to secretly get you into Israel, I believe I can arrange to spend time with you there. At this time, that's all I can tell you about it."

"That's good enough for now. Please tell me that you're not married or engaged or have a steady girlfriend."

Joel laughed. "No, there is no one special, honestly. I've just never found the right woman."

"Till now?"

"Yes, till now."

They sat down together on the sofa and continued to talk. After awhile, Carol slid over and over and gave Joel a light kiss on his cheek.

"That's for saving my life and risking yours to do it.

Joel smiled and asked: "What do I get for saving Robert's life?"

Carol laughed. "That's between you and Robert, but please save the kisses for me."

Joel took her into his arms, and she willingly went there. He kissed her, at first softly and then harder. It seemed to him as if she melted into his body. He had never felt anything like this, and neither had she. After a few minutes of passionate kissing, Joel slid his hand on to one of Carol's breasts. She offered no resistance. He deftly unbuttoned her blouse and pulled it down across her shoulders and off on to the pillow behind her. Joel continued to kiss her and feel her breasts for several minutes.

"You are so patient," she said.

"You are worth waiting for, and I want everything to be perfect," he responded.

She said nothing. He reached behind her and unhooked her rear bra strap. Then he pulled her bra down and off. Joel took a long look at Carol. He could not help but think that she was almost too good to be true: pretty, nice, Jewish, with the best body he had ever seen, and they really connected with each other. "Actually," he thought, "I think I'm in love with her."

Carol was almost in a trance, but her thought processes were clear enough for her to realize that she was in love. She wondered how that could happen so quickly, but at the moment she cared only about those strong feelings she had. Nothing else mattered. She realized that she barely knew him and that she wasn't even sure that the name he had given her, Simon True, was his real name. She also realized that she had no idea what kind of job he worked at, where he lived, or whether he was married, even though he had told her that he was single. All she knew about him was that he had been brought in to help her by Sam Cohen. Then she realized that she didn't know Sam Cohen that well, but she had to trust both Sam and Simon because her life depended on them. The bottom line was that none of that mattered right now because she was totally into the moment and she was in love, no matter how she had gotten there or who this man really was.

His soft touch on her bare breasts was both soothing and exhilarating . She wished the moment would never stop. Carol reached over and pulled on his shirt. He briefly pulled away from her and took his shirt off. The sight of his heavily muscled torso implored Carol to pull her body against his. She did so and felt his hard muscles against her breasts.

Carol was not very experienced in sex because she had never encouraged the men who had dated her, but she had enough experience to know that this was very special. His touch was electric. The combination of pleasure and pain was intense. She could only lay back against the sofa as Joel continued to love her. When they finished, they quietly held each other for several minutes.

Carol said: "Tell me you'll never leave me."

"I would have to be crazy to leave you, and I'm not crazy. I was going to save your life for you, but now I am going to do it for both of us."

Carol smiled and kissed him hard. She believed him.

Chapter 31

The Republican candidate for President of the United States was Leo Short, who came from a lower middle class family in Los Angeles. Born 60 years ago to a laundry driver and his bookkeeper wife, Short excelled in high school and earned a political science degree with honors at the University of Southern California. He majored in political science because he thought it fit well with the law degree he intended to pursue. He accepted a partial scholarship to Yale Law School, was a member of the Law Review Board, and graduated near the top of his class.

Upon graduation, Leo accepted a one year clerkship with a federal judge in Washington, D.C. and became interested in politics. When he finished his clerkship, he spent a few years at a Philadelphia law firm, ran for the U.S. Senate, and was elected as a Republican. Leo spent many years building a power base within the Republican Party until some of the party higher-ups asked him to run for president. Leo accepted, and he defeated three other potential presidential nominees to carry the party's banner against President Rock.

Leo Short believed in free enterprise, individual rights, and states rights, and he was a fiscal conservative. He was a strong supporter of Israel. Leo was a moderate who differed from the party conservatives by favoring at least limited abortion rights and by being against more religion in public schools. He was very much against a path to citizenship for illegal aliens because he believed such a path rewarded an illegal act.

Even though he had locked up the Republican nomination, the convention had yet to convene, so Short still had to pick his running mate. The powerful conservative wing of the party expected him to choose a conservative running mate to balance the ticket, but that was a problem for Short because he disagreed with many of their positions. On the other hand, conservatives made up a substantial percentage of the party, as was evidenced by the large number of votes his more conservative opponents had garnered in the southern states during the primaries. The stakes were large and he knew that his choice of a running mate could make or break his campaign.

Short was a wily politician, and he knew that the available list of running mates included right wing conservatives, Latins, Blacks, Jews and women. The possibilities were almost endless. He remembered that when John McCain selected far right lady governor Sarah Palin, the choice satisfied the party conservatives, but proved disastrous to McCain because most everyone other than conservative voters used Palin as a rallying cry to vote for his opponent. Short needed the moderate and independent votes if he hoped to win. Thus, he sat down with his strategists to consider the best course of action. They jointly agreed that it was unnecessary to select a far right conservative because the conservatives had to vote for him in large numbers anyway. Hard line conservatives simply hated Rock and would vote for almost anyone who could defeat him.

Leo Short considered President Rock to have little substance. Rock attracted people to him as a rock star would, but Rock and his advisers simply had no experience running a large, complex organization. Short believed that they were semi-competent at best and, as such, were dangerous to the United States. He was astonished that so many people could actually vote for Rock. Still, Short recognized that Rock could get a large audience to cheer for him and attract huge campaign contributions, even when he said nothing of substance. That was a skill to be respected, and the liberal press backed Rock no matter what he said.

Short found President Rock difficult to pin down in the one debate they had. No matter the issue, Rock had an answer for why he had or had not done something as President. Frequently the answer did not satisfy the question, but it was close enough to get him off the hook. If nothing else, Rock was a crafty debater who could make facts against him appear to favor his position. Short called Rock's ability to shift the meaning of facts as "making the facts dance," and Rock was a master at blaming the Republicans for everything that went wrong.

At their only debate thus far, Short argued that Rock wanted to push the United States into socialism, that he encouraged powerful unions because their members tended to vote for Democrats, that Rock constantly apologized to our enemies while failing to strongly support Israel, and that he wanted to legalize more and more poor people as citizens because they would likely vote for Democrats in the hope of getting larger welfare payments and free healthcare. Short argued that these policies would change the United States from its capitalist origins to a socialistic country that would be doomed to fail and be crushed under mountains of debt. Instead of responding to Short's direct attacks, Rock sidestepped them by continuously attacking the Republican Party's anti-abortion, pro-religion in the schools, and anti-illegal alien stances.

Thus, the battle lines were drawn. It was up to the voters to determine the direction of the country. If Short was correct, the voters would be deciding the fate of the United States.

The election promised to be close and, in such a close election, perhaps the most important block of votes would be the historically liberal Jews. While Jews made up a small percentage of the United States, they tended to vote in large numbers. Moreover, the key to the election could lie with Florida's 29 electoral votes, more than ten percent of the total electoral votes needed to elect the President, in a state where around 400,000 Jews resided, more than seventy percent of whom had previously voted for Rock. This time around, however, the Jewish support for Rock was less certain because of a broad perception among Jewish voters that Rock's Middle East policies were harmful to Israel.

If the CD of Rock's overture to Israel's Middle East enemies became public, it could cost him the election.

Chapter 32

Although neither party had yet held its convention, both presidential candidates had their ads going full force. Usually there were few, if any, surprises, but this time there was a shocker, at least to Israel. President Rock made an announcement that he is pushing hard behind the scenes for a resolution of the Middle East problem, that he has a plan but that he won't reveal it yet, and that he personally guarantees it will be successful if he is re-elected. He pointed out that the Arab countries have already reduced their anti-American rhetoric, and that those countries would be friendly to the United States in the future under Rock's presidency.

While the Republicans blew Rock's announcement off as a bunch of baloney, the Israeli government was very concerned about that announcement for three reasons. First, President Rock had thus far done nothing whatsoever to involve Israel in any kind of solution to the Middle East issues. Second, it was true that the governments that opposed the very existence of Israel had toned down their anti-American language. Third, the Israeli government had its personality analyst, Mark Corman, analyze Rock's Middle East speech, and Corman concluded that President Rock was telling the truth. Thus, the Israeli government was more than concerned that Rock planned to do something that would adversely impact the State of Israel. That conclusion fit with the apparent secret meeting of Middle East bigwigs in Washington. Even more frightening, until the government could find out what Rock was planning, they could neither prepare for it nor do anything about it.

Chapter 33

After taking Carol Norman to the Israeli Embassy, Joel Drummond began to feel weary. For the past few days, he had been running around with little chance to sleep. Although he was in great physical condition, he needed a full night's sleep, so he borrowed a room at the Embassy. He was anticipating a very hectic day beginning early the next morning. He could have visited Carol at the Embassy, but he concluded that he needed sleep more than he needed sex.

Joel's alarm rang at 5:30AM. He took a short shower, quickly dressed, and grabbed a small breakfast in the cafeteria. Then it was time to go. It was still fairly early, so traffic was reasonably light as Joel again headed for Richmond. He pulled into the parking lot, turned off the engine, and entered the rear door of the Synagogue. Robert and Rabbi BenAmi were waiting for him. Robert had been told only that he was being moved again, but he had no idea where he was going.

"Good morning, Robert. Are you packed and ready to go?"

"Yes, but where am I going and for how long?"

"This will be a permanent move, and you are going to Israel."

Robert had a puzzled expression while the information sank in. A few seconds later, he began to grasp the reality of a permanent move to Israel.

"I don't want to move to Israel and that's final!"

"That's fine, Robert. The choice is yours, but I think you had better consider the consequences of your decision. Other than Israel, there is nowhere I can take you that is really safe for you. If you stay in the United States, the President's men will almost certainly find you and kill you. I can't let you stay with Rabbi BenAmi any longer because it's too risky for him. Most governments will cooperate with President Rock in looking for you and shipping you back to him. The one place you can go where he would never think to look for you is Israel. I had to use very highly placed connections to get you safely out of the United States and into Israel. That's the best I can do for you. If you refuse to go, you are completely on your own."

"You're just trying to get what I have about President Rock's plan for Israel, and it won't work."

"No, Robert, you're wrong. Israel would like to have your information and may need it, but I have not promised to get it as a condition to you moving to Israel. I have never asked you for it and I never will."

"Then why are you getting me to Israel and why would Israel protect me?"

"The answer is simple. While you are not Jewish, you are in trouble because you know about someone who is trying to harm Israel and that person wants to kill because you know his secret. You are in danger because of Israel, so Israel has an ethical obligation to protect you. In a way, you are one with Israel. Even though the Palestinians want the world to believe otherwise, Israel is a refuge for the oppressed and the unfairly hunted, and that includes you."

Robert smiled and said: "It's hard to believe that there is nothing in it for you or for Israel."

"Well, Robert, that's the way it is. Neither Israel nor I is asking anything from you, but I need your answer now because I have to go."

"When can I return to the United States?"

"I'm afraid that you won't be safe here before the election, and probably not while President Rock is in office. Depending on what you know, he may always consider you to be a threat to his reputation, even after he is out of office. To be totally safe, you may have to spend the rest of your life in Israel. Only you know why he wants to kill you."

"Can I have a few minutes to talk to Rabbi BenAmi privately?"

"Yes, but I must leave within the next thirty minutes with you or without you."

Robert left with Rabbi BenAmi. They went to the kitchen while

Joel remained in the Rabbi's office.

"Rabbi, I trust you. We're both black. What should I do?"

"This is a personal decision, so you really need to decide for yourself. You life is in the balance, and I think that Mr. True stated the facts very well. You need to consider whether or not you believe that you can survive on your own."

"I doubt it, but is living in Israel really living for me?"

"Oh yes, I think so. There are even black Ethiopian communities there ."

"Are they Jews?"

"Mostly, yes. Many of them come from families that have practiced Judaism for hundreds, perhaps even thousands, of years. Of course, there are also many Christians in Israel and it is a beautiful and friendly country. I believe that you'll like it."

"Alright, but I have a favor to ask of you."

"What can I do for you, Robert?"

"I want you to hold the reason why President Rock wants to kill me. It's a CD. I want you to promise me that you won't tell anyone that you have it, not even Mr. True. Also I need your promise that you won't listen to it. You will never release it unless I tell you to or unless you learn that I am dead. If you find out that I am dead, you are to give the CD to Sam Cohen of the Jerusalem Post in Washington. Do you agree to do those things for me?"

"Yes, Robert, if that's what you want."

"Here it is. Yes that's what I want. Hide it well. Thank you, Rabbi for keeping me here. I'm surprised, but I'll miss you."

The Rabbi took it from Robert and nodded affirmatively. Robert went to the guest bedroom, picked up his small packed bag, and returned to meet Joel in the office. Robert said he was ready to go to Israel. Joel opened a bag and took out a wig and some other items.

"Before we go, Robert, we need to change your appearance so that no one can recognize you, and you have to agree that you will never tell anyone about me or that you are in Israel."

"I agree."

After Robert had his rapid, but complete, makeover, he looked in the mirror and laughed.

Joel handed a passport to him.

"You have a new name, Cecil Issacs. We have to hurry. Are you ready to go?"

"Yes, I'm ready."

Both Robert and Joel shook hands with Rabbi BenAmi and thanked him. Then they turned and walked out of the Synagogue door and into the parking lot.

Chapter 34

It seemed to Joel as if he was riding on the end of a pendulum: going from Washington to Richmond, then back to Washington, then to the Israeli Embassy, then back to Richmond, now to the airport, and then back to the Israeli Embassy. "Well," he thought, "it is almost over." Robert was well hidden on the floor of the car for the ride to the private airport where the chartered El-Al aircraft awaited the departing trade mission increased by Robert, Carol, and, finally, Joel, although Joel's job would not be completed until he placed his two charges in their appointed places in Israel.

When Joel and Robert reached the airport, Joel presented Robert's Israeli passport and El-Al airline credentials to the Israeli Embassy representative so that the representative could vouch for Robert and so that Robert could board the plane as a flight attendant. The process went smoothly and Robert boarded the aircraft.

Next, Joel left for the Israeli Embassy to collect Carol. First, however, he dropped his rental car off at a rental agency office near the Embassy. Then he walked to the Embassy. Carol was packed and ready, but she was surprised to learn that she would be disguised as a man and that she would receive her permanent Israeli passport after she cleared Israeli customs. All necessary precautions were being taken to ensure that neither Robert nor Carol could be traced to Israel.

When Carol looked into the mirror and saw herself as a man, she laughed out loud.

"Not bad. I'll bet I could attract lots of women, Simon."

"I prefer you as a woman."

"Am I going to learn more about you, Simon?"

"Yes, but that will wait until you are safely in Israel. Let's go."

They went to the airport in an unmarked Embassy car. With the help of the Embassy representative, he escorted Carol onto the plane. There was only one class of service on the charter, but the plane was only a quarter full, so Carol was seated up front, far from everyone else. Joel had instructed her to avoid talking and, if anyone approached her, she was to whisper that she had laryngitis and was told by a doctor not to talk. Joel sat alone at the back of the plane so that no one would connect him to Carol.

Finally, the pre-flight announcements began and everyone was told to fasten their seatbelts. The plane backed out of the blocks and then taxied toward the runway. Since this was a governmental mission from Israel to the United States that used a private airport, there was no other airplane ground traffic. It was only necessary to await the clearance of surrounding airspace before takeoff. After about ten minutes, the airspace became available and the flight was cleared for takeoff. The jet lumbered down the runway and easily lifted off with its light load of passengers, crew, and baggage. Joel let out a silent sigh of relief and settled back in his seat for some well-earned sleep.

Carol also dozed until she was awakened about thirty minutes after takeoff by the captain's announcements. The plane had reached its initial cruising altitude, the air time until landing in Israel would be about eleven hours, the skies were clear, and the flight was expected to be smooth. The captain turned the seat belt sign off and said that everyone could move around the cabin.

Just as Carol began to doze again, she felt a tap on her shoulder and heard someone ask her if she would like dinner. She looked up directly at the flight attendant's name tag which read: Cecil Issacs. Then she looked at the flight attendant and she thought he looked familiar. Suddenly she realized why he was familiar to her, and she gasped "Rob" before stopping. She realized that Robert Johnson was in disguise.

The passengers ate a dinner that was good for an airline: kosher wine, kosher chicken, rolls, and dessert. After dinner, a movie was available, but most of the passengers slept. The flight was smooth as the captain had predicted. When the sun broke through in the morning, the orthodox Jewish passengers faced east and prayed. Breakfast was served followed by the singing of Jewish songs. Robert was mystified by the events, but he thought that if he was going to be an Israeli, even a Christian Israeli, he would learn about the Jewish rituals. He smiled to himself and recognized that he was starting to think a little like an Israeli. Although Carol had been a non-practicing Jew, she recognized much of the process.

As the flight descended toward the airport, Robert got his first look at Israel. He was surprised at how beautiful it appeared. He thought that perhaps Rabbi BenAmi was correct and that he would like it. He certainly hoped so.

When the plane landed, it taxied to its gate at the terminal. Everyone disembarked from the plane, picked up their checked luggage, and lined up for Israeli customs. Joel showed his credentials and arranged for Robert and Carol to move easily through Israeli customs and join Joel at a private car. Once in the car, Robert and Joel laughed at the way Carol looked as a man, and then Joel told them where each of them was going.

Chapter 35

Ever since he had investigated the death of John Davis, Sergeant Donald Hammond of the District of Columbia Police Department had been bothered by something about the death. It was closed as a drug overdose, but Hammond thought there was something decidedly unkosher about it. He just couldn't put his finger on what was nagging in the back of his brain about the case.

Now, several days after the death, when Hammond was thinking of nothing in particular, the reason for his discomfort popped into his mind—it was that there were three deaths the same day, all linked in one way or another to the White House. Yes, that was it! He pondered, on the other hand, what did it mean? There was the death of a twelve year boy who apparently fell off a roof nearly next door to the White House, an unexplained explosion killing a white House employee, and the death of a White house staffer of an apparent drug overdose. What, if any, could the connection be? He didn't know, but three deaths connected to the White House in one day was highly unusual and very suspicious.

Hammond went into the files and pulled the reports on all three deaths. There was nothing to suggest foul play, except perhaps in the death of Robert Johnson, but there was nothing concrete to rule out murder. The father of the deceased twelve year old boy had said that his son frequently was on that roof and knew better than to lean over the edge. Hammond wondered what the boy could have seen that would have caused him to lean over the edge. In the case of Davis, he had no history of prior drug use and no reason to be in the area where his body was discovered.

It was all very strange, perhaps too strange to be a coincidence.

Sergeant Hammond knocked on the open door of his boss,

Lieutenant Ferdie Robbins. Robbins looked up at Hammond and told him to come in but did not invite him to sit down.

"What is it, Hammond? You know I'm busy, so get on with it."

"Sir, I have a problem with three deaths and I think they need further investigation."

Robbins asked for details and Hammond explained who the subjects were and why he was bothered by the deaths. Robbins leaned back and thought for a few moments.

"Hammond, there you go tilting at windmills like Don Quixote again. You're a good cop and you would have been a lieutenant years ago if you didn't keep coming up with these harebrained ideas. This is the White House you're talking about investigating, man. Are you crazy? You have no evidence of a crime here, just a hunch, and you want to go and stir up the White House staff and security. What in the hell are you smoking?"

"Well, sir, I think something smells and I am sure that the president would like to know if someone murdered some of his people."

"So now you want to investigate the President of the United States? You are crazy!"

"I didn't say that, but I don't know where the investigation may lead. Are you ordering me to lay off?"

"No, Hammond. I never want to be accused of covering up anything, so you do your investigation and get yourself into as much as trouble as you like, but if you find nothing of substance within the next twenty-four hours, I order you to close the investigation. Is that clear?"

"Completely."

"Robbins shook his head in a negative manner and said: "Now get out of here and do your investigation. Keep me up to date on whatever you find, though I doubt that it will be anything."

Hammond left and headed to White House Security, and Robbins phoned his captain to advise him of the investigation. The captain was concerned about an investigation involving the White House, so he phoned the Police Commissioner, who, in turn, phoned the security chief at the White house.

When Sergeant Hammond arrived at White House Security, the staff was waiting for him and they seemed very cooperative. They let him search Robert Johnson's locker and the office of John Davis. He found nothing of interest. When he asked to interview the secretary of John Davis, he was told only that she was not at work that day. There was nothing further he could do at the White House for the moment other than to interview the security staff. He did so, but again learned nothing of value, so he returned to the office.

When he returned, he was told to report to Lieutenant Robbins' office immediately. He reported to Robbins, who greeted him with a smile.

"Well, Hammond, you're just the man I'm looking for. You've finally hit the jackpot."

"What do you mean, Lieutenant?"

Robbins laughed. "Boy have you hit the jackpot. Effective immediately, you're on temporary assignment to the undercover narcotics squad of the Seattle Police Department. They need someone who the local narcs don't know and you're it, you lucky guy."

"What are you talking about? The Seattle Police Department? Is this a joke?"

"It's no joke, Hammond. Here's your plane ticket. Your plane leaves in three hours so you'd better get going. I know it's a long flight, but you're flying coach. The Seattle Police Department doesn't have the funds for first class."

"I'm a homicide detective. I don't know anything about narcotics, and undercover sounds like dangerous work."

"It is dangerous work. I guess you'll just have to learn on the job. I hear the women are good looking in Seattle, so you should have a good time."

"How long is this assignment?"

"Initially, for a year, but it could be extended."

"A year or more! I won't go!"

"That's your choice, but the order came from the Commissioner's office, so my guess is that if you refuse you'll be retired. You can't fight with the big boss and win, so suit yourself."

"I guess I have to go."

"That's right. Here is your plane ticket. I understand it rains a lot in Seattle, so don't forget your umbrella."

Hammond took the ticket and left the office. As he walked down the hall to the exit, he heard the echoes of laughter coming from Robbins and his squad. He wondered whether this transfer was because of his White House investigation. He concluded that it was.

Chapter 36

Joel Drummond elected to first deposit Robert Johnson at his new home and to drop Carol Norman off later, so Carol accompanied Robert and Joel on their journey to the country. After about a forty minute drive, Joel turned the car down a small road for a few hundred yards and then he stopped. In front of them was a beautiful kibbutz with trees and flowers. The sign read Peta Tikva.

They all got out of the car and walked a short way to a large building, and they went inside. An attractive black woman greeted them and introduced herself as Hannah Thomas. She was very friendly as Robert, now known as Cecil Isaacs, Carol, and Joel, still using the name Simon True, introduced themselves. She addressed Cecil.

"Cecil, we've been expecting you, and I'm here to welcome you to your new home in the State of Israel. This kibbutz has mostly Ethiopian Jews, but some of us were born in the United States. I was born in Memphis and I have been living in Peta Tikva for the past six years. I love it! It's clean, friendly, and beautiful, and the people are some of the nicest I have ever met."

Cecil looked a little puzzled. "Are you Jewish, Hannah?"

"Oh yes, I am very Jewish. I was raised as a Southern Baptist, but I got interested in Judaism in college and when I converted to Judaism I moved here to really experience the religion. The change to the communal living we have here took a bit of getting used to at first, but it was worth the effort. I will help you get through the transition and I'll teach you enough Hebrew to get by."

"I'm Christian," Cecil said a little defensively. "Is that a problem?"

"Not at all. There are many thousands of Christians and Muslims in Israel and several Christians in Peta Tikva. Unlike Christianity, the Jewish religion does not believe in trying to convert people; however, if you ever decide on your own that you want to convert, you can do so. The choice is completely yours. The Christians in our kibbutz hold church services most Sundays, so if you want to attend I can put you in touch with them."

"I was not observant at home, so I probably won't go to church here either. What does everyone do here all day?"

"Well, Cecil, everyone contributes to the community in some way here. We have lots of farming jobs, we make small electrical items for use here and sale to other communities, and we have people who clean and bake. You can take a few days to look around and decide what you would like to do."

"Will you go around with me and show me the ropes?"

"Certainly, Cecil, for as long as you need me."

Cecil couldn't help but think that she was attractive, smart, and personable, so he may "need" her for a long time. He really liked her.

For the next twenty minutes, Hannah, Cecil, Joel, and Carol sat, talked, and drank fresh lemonade, which Cecil thought was the best lemonade he had ever tasted. Finally, Joel and Carol left Cecil in the apparently expert care of Hannah, and drove toward Jerusalem. Cecil had mixed emotions about their leaving. On one hand, he was comfortable with them, and on the other hand he wanted some private time with Hannah.

Hannah took Cecil on a tour of the kibbutz. He was surprised at how large and beautiful it was. Hannah introduced Cecil to many people, all of whom were very friendly. He tried the food in the cafeteria and it turned out to be very good, although there were some foods he had never heard of before. After awhile, Cecil began to feel tired since he had only limited sleep on the plane and he was now in a far different time zone than the one he had left in the United States, so Hannah took him to his new home.

Cecil's house was small, but larger than the now destroyed apartment where he used to live in Washington, D.C. It had a living room, a kitchen, a bathroom and a bedroom. Each room was heated and air-conditioned by a reverse cycle room air conditioner. The refrigerator was filled with food and Cecil smiled when he noticed the vase of flowers on his dining room table. Everything that he needed had been attended to. He flopped down on the bed and fell asleep.

Chapter 37

Peter grabbed his cell phone almost as soon as it had begun to ring. The caller was a Washington, D.C. policeman. Looking for Carol Norman's car required more manpower than Peter had at his disposal, so the District of Columbia police, as well as the police of all other major cities in the United States, had been alerted to watch for it. The policeman reported that he had found it parked in the parking lot at the main bus station. It had probably been parked there for several days, according to the policeman. Peter wrote down the car's location and left for the bus station.

When he arrived, Peter located the car and carefully used a special tool to open the door. He put on gloves and carefully searched the car and then the car trunk. He found nothing of interest, so he phoned his fingerprint team and told them to come to the bus station. The specialists arrived in less than half an hour and went over the car completely. They examined many fingerprints, but all of them ultimately turned out to be Carol's. There was nothing to suggest that anyone other than Carol had been in the car. Carol had done a good job of eradicating Robert's prints.

Peter ordered the fingerprint crew to sample the prints in Carol's house, although he doubted that they would find anything. Since there had been no evidence thus far that Carol was with anyone else, Peter had tentatively concluded that Carol was alone when she disappeared. Therefore, he decided that checking every print in Carol's house would be a waste of resources, so checking a sample of prints would suffice. As to the car, he decided to leave it in place, but under a 24 hour watch, in case Carol came back to retrieve it. He also assigned two men to check bus rosters for the past several days and to interview bus drivers and other personnel. If she had simply gotten onto a subway car or walked onto a train, there would be no way to trace her.

The fingerprint crew checked about a third of the prints throughout Carol's house and reported to Peter that they found only Carol's prints there. Carol's luck held because the crew had missed the few prints of Robert that she had missed removing. Peter would have felt more secure if the crew had found some other prints in the house, perhaps those of a friend, but he reasoned that Carol lived alone so she probably did her socializing elsewhere. He concluded it was highly probable that Carol had disappeared alone and without help, so she would most likely make a mistake and be located sooner or later. After all, his people were much better at finding someone than an amateur would be at avoiding being found.

He phoned President Rock and briefed him. President Rock was not happy that Carol had evaded capture thus far.

"Dammit, Peter, how could it have taken so long to find the car in such a public place?"

"I don't know. We don't have the staff to check everywhere, so we asked for an assist from the D.C. police. Unless the car just got there, they should have found it more quickly."

"So what you're telling me is that you've lost her. Is that right?"

"I'm afraid so, but we think we'll find her pretty soon since the evidence is strong that she got away without help."

"She certainly has done a good job of staying out of sight so far. The only good news is since she hasn't been quoted yet as saying anything about my Middle East meeting, she probably doesn't know anything. This Robert Johnson is another matter. He's dangerous and we need to find him. Could he be with the girl?"

"We don't think that is likely, Mr. President. We have nothing whatsoever linking the two of them together. So far as we know, they've never even met."

"Alright, but keep on this."

"Yes sir."

President Rock walked to his wife's office and told her about his conversation with Peter.

She snarled and said: "Your security people are a bunch of stupid, incompetent assholes. You should probably have them hit." President Rock shrugged, turned, and went back to his office. He leaned back in his chair and thought that while his wife may not have been serious, she may have been correct.

Sometime later, Peter received a phone call telling him that Carol bought no ticket in her name and no one remembered seeing her at the bus station. Peter thought that Carol had certainly done a good job of disappearing, especially for a woman who was without help. Still, there was nothing to suggest otherwise. Perhaps she just had dumb luck on her side.

Chapter 38

When Joel reached Jerusalem, he turned the car toward the King David Hotel. He gave the car to the valet and took Carol to the King's Garden Restaurant. The magnificent King David was perhaps the most famous hotel in Jerusalem. While Joel would have preferred to take Carol to the hotel's La Regence-Grill Room, it did not open until dinner time and Joel was not sure that Carol would be able to stay awake that long. Instead, they went to the King's Garden, which overlooked the garden and the pool. It was a beautiful setting for lunch.

The two of them made small talk while they enjoyed the excellent food, but when the check came, Carol broached the subject of what happens next.

"Carol, you will have an apartment in the Arnona section of Jerusalem. It is an upscale, but not overly expensive, quiet area. I'll give you a little history of the neighborhood. When we fought the War of Independence after the State of Israel was founded in 1948, Jordanian and Egyptian troops took over the area and the Jews hurriedly left. Well now, all these years later, Arnona is a popular place. I think you'll really like it."

"It sounds nice, but how do I pay for it?"

"The government will pay for the first two months, so you will need to find a job in order to pay your own way after that. Don't look so puzzled. You are an experienced English speaking secretary, so you will be in demand. I'll have an employment agency contact you tomorrow if that's ok with you."

"Yes, that's fine. I would like to begin to fit in here as quickly as possible. Now I have another question: what is your real name and who are you?"

"Ah, yes, I think it is time for me to answer that. My real name is Joel Drummond. Actually that is the name I use in business and everybody calls me by that name. I was born Joel Dror. I use the name Drummond because I run an international food brokering business and Dror is a rather ethnic name that could result in anti-Jewish sentiment in some of the countries where my business operates. The business is called Middle East Foods."

"So, Joel, and I like that name better than Simon, you were able to get us on a trade mission flight because you're in the business."

"Yes, I have some very good connections. My father, Louis, started the business after moving here from Chicago. I was born here, so I speak both English and Hebrew as well as a few other languages I use in business. My business is headquartered in Jerusalem and I live here when I'm not on the road. I'm 41 years old and I've never been married because I've spent all of my time with the business so far. That's about it for me. How about you?"

"I'm 36 years old and I've never been married, probably because no one ever asked me." She laughed. "Seriously, I've just never found the right person. As I told you before, my mother is Jewish and my father has no religion. We didn't practice any religion when I was growing up, and, while I think of myself as being Jewish, I've never really practiced anything. My parents teach history at a junior college in Madison, Wisconsin, where I was born, so I guess we are sort of neighbors since Madison and Chicago are only a two hour drive apart. By now, I'm sure my parents are worried about me. Can I tell them where I am?"

"I advise against that. You can bet that President Rock's people almost certainly have your parents under surveillance and are probably monitoring their phone calls too. Is there some code word no one else knows that would let your parents know you're alright?"

"Actually, there is," she beamed. "When I was a child, my parents would call me 'Shilley" because they would threaten to trade me in at Shilley's Department Store for another little girl if I was bad. I'm sure they remember it."

"Is Shilley's still in business?"

"Yes."

"Good. I'll arrange for someone at Shilley's to phone them and tell them that Shilley's is great and tell them to shop there. Do you think they would understand the message?"

"Yes, I'm quite certain they would. My parents always played word games, so they would understand that they are getting a secret message from me and they wouldn't ask any questions. Can you really arrange that?"

"I think so. Anyway I'll try it. You look rather tired. Let's go to your apartment."

Carol nodded in agreement and they left. They drove to Arnona, which Carol thought was lovely, and arrived at Carol's new apartment. They went inside. The apartment was small, but very nice. It had a good sized living room, a small kitchen, a bedroom, and a single bathroom. All in all, she thought she would feel quite at home there once she got used to being in Israel.

"Before I forget, I need to give your new identification papers and passport to you. Your name is now Rachel Klein. You can give me the old passport showing you as a man."

Carol, now Rachel, laughed and handed the male passport to Joel She said: "I suppose that we'll have to get used to calling each other by our new names. Would you like to stay for awhile?"

"I think it's best if I leave. You look very tired from the stress of the past few days and the overnight flight, and I'm pretty tired too. I also need to check in at the office."

"Joel, you're not trying to get rid of me now that we're in Israel, are you?"

"Not a chance, I just believe we both need some rest. How about if I pick you up around 6:00PM for dinner tomorrow?"

"Absolutely."

"Great. Here is my card with my contact phone numbers. I've also written my home number on it. That should reach me at any time.

Until tomorrow, then."

Joel gave Rachel a big kiss and then turned and left. It wasn't that she didn't trust him, but she dialed the office phone number on his card.

The answer was first in Hebrew and then in English: "Middle East Foods. Can I help you?"

"Joel Drummond, please."

"Mr. Drummond is out of town, but I expect him back either today or tomorrow. Can I help you or would you prefer to leave a message?"

"Neither, thank you. I'll call back later."

Next, she dialed his cell phone.

"Joel Drummond."

"Oh, Joel, this is Rachel and I just wanted to hear your voice. I can hardly wait to see you tomorrow."

"Me too Rachel."

When they hung up, he smiled.

Chapter 39

Cecil was up early the next morning. He made some breakfast. He didn't know what all of the foods were, so he tried some different things. All in all, he found the foods strange, but tasty. He took a shower, got dressed, and then found an English language news station on his small TV. There was nothing of interest, but it helped pass the time until he dozed off in the chair. He dreamed about President Rock, explosions, and a bird with Shirley's face. He asked the bird why it had his deceased girl friend's face, but before he got an answer there was a knock on his door that awakened him.

Hannah was at the door when Cecil opened it. She looked rather attractive, and Cecil smiled and told her to come in.

"It's 9:00AM already, Cecil, and it's a beautiful, sunny day. It's time to get moving. Unless you have something better to do, I'm going to show you Jerusalem. Have you ever been there before?"

"No, but I've seen pictures of some of the Christian sites, so I'd sure like to see Jerusalem."

"Good. Have you had breakfast?"

"Yes."

"Then let's go."

When they arrived in Jerusalem, Hannah parked the car and took Cecil to a tour office. There was a bus almost ready to leave, and Hannah presented two tickets to the driver. She and Cecil boarded. She let him take the window seat so that he could get a better view.

"Where did you get the tickets, Hannah?"

"Compliments of the Israeli government. I was given these as soon as we knew you were coming. It's pretty much standard for a new resident of Israel, especially if you haven't been here before. Now it's time to sit back and enjoy the tour. By the way, it's in English."

The tour guide took the microphone. "Ladies and Gentlemen, we are about to depart. During this tour, you will see many of the most famous sites in Jerusalem. The tour is structured in the order that I would like you to see the sites rather than which ones are close to each other, so we may be driving back and forth. My wife thinks I'm a little crazy anyway, so please forgive the unique way I like to do the tour."

"The old city of Jerusalem is divided into four quarters: the Jewish Quarter, the Christian Quarter, the Moslem Quarter, and the Armenian Orthodox Quarter. These four quarters have been in existence since the days of the Ottoman Empire. The Jewish Quarter has been home to Jews since ancient times except when the Romans expelled the Jews. While Jews lived pretty much in peace with the other residents of the city for many years, during the 1948 War of Independence the Jordanian Army captured it and held it until it was recaptured by the Israeli Army 1967. While it was under Jordanian control, almost every building in the Jewish Quarter was destroyed, including nearly all of the Synagogues. Therefore, the architecture of the Quarter is almost completely from the late 1960's and 1970's."

The guide continued to comment on the Jewish Quarter until the bus reached Zion Square. The Square, he explained, is a major center of West Jerusalem. Is is constantly loaded with people of all kinds, from police to tour groups. The guide explained some of its history, both positive and negative, all while the tour bus inched past teenagers and street musicians.

The passengers next learned about the Damascus Gate, which divides Jerusalem's old city from East Jerusalem. The Damascus Gate, referred to by the Arabs as Bab Al-Amud, is the heart of the Arab part of Jerusalem. Contrasting with the Damascus Gate is the Jaffe Gate, which separates West Jerusalem from the Old City.

The next two sites held particular interest for Cecil, and he paid close attention to that part of the tour. The street of Via Dolorosa covers the last walk of Jesus, after he was convicted by the Romans, to Golgotha where he was crucified. The first nine Stations of the Cross are located along Via Dolorosa: the beating of Jesus, the remains of the Arch of Ecce Homo, where Jesus first fell, where Jesus met his mother, Simon of Cyrene's encounter with Jesus, the place where Veronica wiped Jesus' face, the second place where Jesus fell, the place where the pious woman met Jesus, and the place where Jesus fell for the third time.

The remaining five Stations of the Cross are located inside the Church of the Holy Sepulchre, the next stop on the tour. That church, in the Christian Quarter, is a very important place for Catholic and Christian Orthodox pilgrims. It was built on the supposed spot of the Golgotha, where Jesus was crucified, and the tomb of Jesus, from which he was resurrected. The guide went into considerable detail about how Constantine had the church built. Cecil was thrilled by the opportunity to go inside.

The tour continued to the Dome of the Rock, the Muslim shrine which is often shown as the symbol of Jerusalem, the Tower of David Museum, the center of the government of Israel, the Knesset, and the Mount of Olives, which leads down to the Western Wall.

The Western Wall, or Wailing Wall, is from the Second Temple, and it is considered the holiest place in the world to Jews. It is the place, according to the Kabbalah, where God is present and prayers are answered. People come from all over the world to place a written request or a prayer for health within the cracks in the stones. It lies at the foot of the western side of the Temple Mount. After the 1948 War of Independence, the Wall came under control of Jordan, and for 19 years Jews were barred from the site until Israel liberated it in 1967. Cecil watched with fascination the many different kinds people praying at the Wall. Some prayed standing straight up while others bobbed up and down. Cecil had never seen anything like it.

The guide made an announcement: "Our final stop will be at Yad Vashem. Before we get there, I'd like to tell you about one of the important holidays in Israel, Yom Hazikaron, which is Israel's Remembrance Day. It occurs in the Spring, and it commemorates soldiers who died and those who were killed by terrorists. There is a ceremony at the Western Wall and a siren is sounded at 8:00PM that evening. On the following morning, a flag and flowers are placed on each grave, and the thousands of bereaved families visit the graves of their loved ones. While Israel is technically at peace, in truth it is in a constant state of war because the countries that surround us frequently state their desire to destroy us or to push us into the sea, and we never know when they will try to carry out their threat. Every day, we are bombarded by rockets from our neighbors. Will a peace treaty with the Palestinians end this threat? It seems unlikely."

The tour ended at Yad Vashem, the powerful memorial to the Jewish victims of the nazi Holocaust. Yad Vashem is a large complex with memorial sites, the Holocaust History Museum, the Hall of Remembrance, the Museum of Holocaust Art, a Synagogue, and other areas. The site includes "The Righteous Among Nations," which commemorates non-Jews who, often at great personal risk, saved Jews during the Holocaust. Cecil was deeply moved by his experience there.

After the tour, Hannah took Cecil to a kosher restaurant. Cecil learned that kosher restaurants have either meat products or dairy products, but not both. Still, he found the food interesting. After lunch, they walked around Jerusalem for an hour or so. Then they returned to the car for their return to Peta Tikva.

"Did you enjoy your day in Jerusalem, Cecil?"

"Wow! I've never seen anything like it. Imagine, all of the famous Christian sites almost next to the famous Jewish and Muslim sites, and all in one city. No wonder people are always fighting over Jerusalem. At least Israel lets everyone come. It's hard to believe that the Jordanians kept the Jews from seeing their own religious sites for 19 years. That was really mean!"

"Yes, that was mean. Now you live here and you can go to Jerusalem any time you want to and see whatever you like. There is so much more to see than what we saw on the tour, so let me know when you want to go back to Jerusalem."

"I will Hannah. Thank you for a beautiful day. I've seen pictures of these places, but I never thought I would see them in person. It's really incredible."

When they reached Peta Tikva, Cecil thanked Hannah and went to his house for a nap.

Although he was still tired from the long flight from Washington, D.C., he couldn't fall asleep. He sat in a chair for a long time. He began to think about the all of the events beginning with his finding the CD and through his wonderful day in Jerusalem. He was too tired to eat, so, finally he went to bed.

Chapter 40

He was in such a state of both physical and mental exhaustion that Cecil slept until he was awakened by a loud knocking at his front door at 10:00AM. He slowly got out of bed and answered the door, still in his pajamas. Hannah greeted him with a smile.

"Cecil, what's the matter with you? It's mid-morning and you're still asleep? That's not the way we do things in Israel."

Cecil mumbled something about being sorry. Hannah laughed.

"I was only joking, Cecil, but you do need to get moving because I'm taking you somewhere very special. We are going to another kibbutz to attend a 1:00 concert by a children's orchestra that will knock your socks off, as kids in the United States would say. Get dressed and I'll pick you up at 12:15."

Cecil took a shower, got dressed, and made some lunch. At 12:15, he was waiting at the front door for Hannah. She arrived right on time and they drove to the kibbutz. When they arrived, they got out of Hannah's car and entered a small auditorium. Most of the seats were already filled, so they sat near the back. At 1:00, a group of teenage children took their positions on the stage and began to play. Cecil could hardly believe how good they were. He was no expert on classical music, but he knew a professional sound when he heard one, and this group sounded professional.

The beautiful music continued for more than an hour, after which all of the attendees were treated to lemonade and cookies. There was a chance to meet the artists. Cecil was surprised to feel almost as wonderful as he had in Jerusalem.

When Cecil and Hannah walked out of the auditorium and into the warm afternoon sun, they both felt very relaxed. Suddenly, their peaceful feelings were shattered by the sounds of explosions very close to them. As the ground shook, Cecil fell. The earth vibrated as if he were in an earthquake, and the loud screeching sound of rockets hurt his ears.

There were only three rockets that hit the field next to the auditorium and the entire incident took only two minutes, but it seemed to Cecil as if the explosions lasted much longer than that. Cecil lay on the ground shaking and grabbing onto the grass. His brain transported him back a few days to the explosion at his Washington apartment. He pictured Shirley laying dead in the demolished apartment, and he cried.

Hannah held Cecil until he stopped crying and shaking. When he regained his composure, Cecil was embarrassed, and he noticed that Hannah's arm was bleeding. Hannah smiled.

"It's alright now, Cecil. The rockets are finished. No one was hurt. Don't worry about my arm because it's just a scratch. That was your first exposure to a Palestinian rocket attack. I'm afraid you'll experience many of them and you will get used to them like the rest of us. It's simply a way of life in Israel. Even most of the moderate Palestinians would like to kill all of us and I doubt that a peace treaty will change that."

Cecil apologized to Hannah for losing his composure, but he said nothing about the Washington explosion or about Shirley. He let Hannah think that he was frightened by experiencing his first rocket attack. Cecil told Hannah he was alright. As they left, they saw Israeli air force planes zoom overhead on their way to the Palestinian border. Hannah drove Cecil to his house.

When he arrived home, Cecil knew it was time for some serious soul searching. The question at issue was what to do about the CD. He felt very conflicted about whether to leave it with Rabbi BenAmi, destroy it, or turn it over to Israel or the press. Whichever he decided, he realized, had major ramifications for peoples and countries.

On one side of the equation were the effects of releasing the CD. Since the plot to destroy Israel was by a black president, releasing the

CD would make blacks look bad and could also destroy the credibility of the United States. It could turn the United States into a country that could not be trusted by its allies. It would almost certainly result in a black president, President Rock, losing the election and having his reputation destroyed. Thus, reasoned Cecil, releasing the CD could have major international consequences.

On the other side of the equation was the existence of Israel, the country that protected him from the black president who had tried to kill him and who had killed his girlfriend and who knows how many other people. In addition, for all Israel had done for Cecil, it had asked for nothing in return and now he was a resident of Israel. Could he let a United States president caught up in his own perceived destiny destroy Israel in partnership with the monsters who fire rockets at Israeli children?

The answer wasn't an easy one, and, in order to give his thinking process a rest, Cecil turned on his TV set and tuned to a European English language news station. After a few minutes, there was a piece of news about the Israeli air force reprisal for the rocket attack Cecil had experienced. There was no mention of the rocket attack on the kibbutz. The only pictures shown were those of crying widows of the Palestinians who had fired the rockets. Cecil turned off the TV in disgust.

Cecil walked to the phone and dialed.

Chapter 41

The phone rang in Richmond, Virginia.

"Rabbi BenAmi. How can I help you?"

"Rabbi, you have something I gave you. Please deliver it now."

"Are you certain you want me to do that?"

Yes, I am certain. Thank you for your help."

Cecil hung up. Rabbi BenAmi located the CD, put it in his pocket, and went to his car. He drove out of the Synagogue parking lot and turned in the direction of Washington. On the way, the Rabbi stopped at a gas station to use the phone. When it was answered, he asked for Sam Cohen.

"This is Sam Cohen."

"Mr. Cohen, you don't know me, but a friend of yours, who will remain unnamed, has asked me to deliver a gift to you. Will you be in your office for another hour or so?"

"What kind of gift are we talking about?"

"I don't know, but I think you recently offered your hospitality to him. Perhaps this gift is for your kindness"

"Yes, maybe it is. Please come to the office. I will wait for you. Tell the receptionist that I said she is to show you to my office immediately."

Rabbi BenAmi hung the phone up, got into his car, and continued his trip to Washington.

Chapter 42

Rabbi BenAmi parked his car and went to the offices of the Jerusalem Post. He told the receptionist that Mr. Cohen asked that he be brought in immediately. The secretary had already been alerted that she was to bring the visitor to Cohen's office without delay. Cohen greeted him at the office door, motioned for the visitor to sit down, and then Cohen closed the door and sat down behind his desk.

Sam Cohen began: "I won't ask who you are because I don't need to know and it may be best if I don't know. When you phoned, you said you have a gift for me. I assume that it's from Robert."

"Before I can answer that, I need to confirm that you are Mr. Cohen since my instructions are to deliver the gift specifically to Mr. Cohen. You probably know why I am being cautious".

Sam Cohen showed Rabbi BenAmi his driver's license and his press card. The Rabbi nodded affirmatively, removed the CD from his pocket, and handed it to Cohen.

"Mr. Cohen, I held this merely for safekeeping. I have not listened to it and I have no idea what is on it. I only know that it has something to do with Israel. I have neither a need nor a desire to hear it now. I'm sure it's in good hands, so I will leave now. If its contents are published in the Jerusalem Post, I will read about in the newspaper."

"Sir, and this is important, did you get this CD directly from Robert Johnson, and has it been only in your possession since then?"

"The answer to both questions is 'yes'."

Rabbi BenAmi turned and left Cohen's office to return to his Synagogue in Richmond. As soon as the Rabbi left, Sam Cohen buzzed his secretary's phone and told her to bring in a CD player as quickly as possible. It took less than five minutes for the player to be delivered.

Sam plugged the player in, inserted the CD, and pushed "play." Sam heard the unmistakable voice of President Rock saying: "Hello everyone. I am sure you want to know why I have invited you here."

Sam's eyes narrowed in concentration as he listened to the full CD. When it finished, he stared at the CD player in disbelief. The words "My God" hissed out of his mouth. He thought that he must have misunderstood what he had heard, so he played the CD again. This time there could be no mistake, he had heard the CD correctly the first time. Sam picked up the phone and dialed an extension.

"Terry, this is Sam. Get your rear end to my office immediately. Don't even stop for a cup of coffee."

Terry Tan was the Post's top man at authenticating anything and everything. He had been doing it for nearly twenty years and he was hardly ever wrong. He burst into Sam Cohen's office.

"My gosh, Sam, what's so all fired important?"

"Take this CD and carefully make one back-up copy. Then put the original through every test you can imagine, maybe even some you can't imagine. I want a hundred percent assurance that this thing is real and that the voice on the CD belongs to President Rock. I want to know if there is even a one percent chance that anything on this could be phony or if this CD could have been spliced together. And one other thing: no one is to know about this or even know that this CD exists. Guard the damn thing with your life, and I mean that!"

As an expert in forensic voice identification, Terry understood that there was more than one way to ensure the voice on the CD was that of President Rock. He used very sophisticated software to match the voice on the CD with archived recordings of the president's speeches. Since the quality of the CD and of the archived speeches was excellent, Terry knew that he could read the comparison with almost perfect accuracy. He tested using biometrics as well as audio enhancement. Then, he manually examined the CD and further enhanced it to check for anything that could mean the CD was edited in any way. When he was done, he took the CD to an anxiously waiting Sam Cohen.

"Sam, I've run every test I know of. In my opinion, the voice is that of President Rock and there is no evidence whatsoever that the disc has been doctored. I was so concentrated on the analysis that I didn't even listen to the content. Is this really hot?"

"Terry, in all of my years in the newspaper business, this is the hottest thing I have ever heard. It can hand the presidential election to Leo Short and it could create one of the biggest political scandals in the history of the United States. I want you to carefully make fifty copies of this and give me a written report repeating your conclusions. I need all of that as fast as you can get it to me. Be very careful to preserve the original CD in exactly the condition it is in now."

"Ok, Sam, I won't leave here until all of that is done."

Chapter 43

Sam phoned Joel Drummond.

"Joel, this is Sam Cohen."

"Hello, Sam. The last time you phoned me in Israel, I ended up with a lot of work and a trip to the United States. I assume this isn't a social call."

"How right you are. This is no social call. Have you talked to our friend Robert lately?"

"No, but I know where he is. Do you need him for something?"

"No. Did he ever tell you what he has that's so important?"

"Not yet, Sam. Why do I feel as if something is going on?"

"Something very big is going on. In fact, the biggest thing I've ever experienced in all my years of reporting. Our friend had a CD delivered to me a short time ago by a chunky black man. I didn't ask his name and he didn't offer it. Do you know who he is?"

"I could make a guess, but I'm not certain. What was on the CD?"

Sam described the contents of the CD and that his expert had authenticated it. Joel could hardly believe what he was hearing, but it seemed to fit well with what he already knew about Middle East government representatives flying to Washington for a meeting from which the Israeli government was excluded.

"What are you going to do with it Sam?"

"I'm going to publish it. It's too big a story to keep to just my newspaper, so I'm having the CD copied and sent to all news services and major newspapers. It will be in the Jerusalem Post tomorrow morning."

"How fast can you send us a copy of the CD?"

"The first copy will be overnighted to you."

"Send one to me and one to the Prime Minister. You have our

addresses. Mark them "Personal and Confidential" and "For the addressee only."

"They'll go out tonight and the two of you will have them tomorrow."

"One other thing, Sam. These guys are dangerous people, so watch your back. Make sure the news services get this before you publish, so that President Rock doesn't know where the CD came from, and send it to the news services anonymously.

"Alright, Joel. I'll do it."

Joel got into his car and drove to the Prime Minister's office. He told the Prime Minister's secretary that he needed to see "the Boss" immediately. He was quickly shown into the office. The Prime Minister motioned for Joel to sit down. Joel briefed the Prime Minister about the phone call from Sam Cohen and about the contents of the CD. The Prime Minister fixed his eyes on the ceiling for several seconds and then looked at Joel.

"Well, Joel, we knew that Rock was probably planning something bad for Israel. Now we know what it is, and it's worse than I had imagined. Now that the cat is out of the bag, what do you think the fallout will be?"

"Sir, I think it will cost Mr. Rock his liberal Jewish funds for re-election, and it has to cost him the Jewish votes he needs so desperately. Without Jewish campaign funds and Jewish votes in key states like New York and Florida, I don't see how he can win a second term."

"Good! Israel can't afford to have Rock as president of the United States for a second term. What should we say to the media?"

Sir, I think we should say nothing until we're asked, and when we're asked I think we should say that we're shocked by the whole thing. Once our people analyze the CD, if we're asked, and we probably will be by the press, we should say we have examined the CD and that it appears to be authentic. Since the Jerusalem Post went over the CD with a fine tooth comb and pronounced it to be authentic, I'm sure our people will concur."

"Yes. I believe your approach makes sense. It's best for Israel to largely stay out of American politics and let the American voters, particularly the Jewish voters, finish off Rock on their own. I'll call a meeting of the Knesset and brief everyone. Keep me posted on anything you find out."

Joel left, got into his car, and drove to Peta Tikva. He knocked on Cecil's front door and Cecil let him into the house.

"Well, Cecil, your CD has caused quite a stir. Just to satisfy my curiosity, why did you release it?"

"My President forced me to move to Israel, so I resent his trying to destroy my new country. Israel took me in without asking for anything in return when I needed help, so I felt that I owed Israel. Is Mr. Cohen going to publish it?"

"Yes and he has sent it to the news services. Are you positive that it's real?"

"Yes. I took it out of a recording device in the media room of the White House after President Rock had a room full of people there. Some of the people wore turbans and robes, you know, like Arabs wear."

"Yes, Cecil, I know. Thank you for making the right decision."

They spoke for awhile. Cecil said that he's getting along well with Hannah's help and that he's slowly getting used to living in Israel. He also described his tour of Jerusalem and his narrow escape from the Palestinian rockets. When they finished, Joel wished Cecil well and returned to Jerusalem.

Chapter 44

There was a banging on President Rock's office door followed by his secretary bursting in.

"Josephine, what in the hell is going on. You can't just run into my office."

"I'm sorry, Mr. President, but this is an emergency. I've got two news services and four reporters on hold wanting to talk to you."

"Tell them I'm busy and transfer them to my Press Secretary. That's what you should have done in the first place."

"You don't understand, Mr. President. They want a statement about that secret meeting you had with the Arabs. They want you to comment on your plans to destroy Israel in your next term."

"What! Oh shit, that asshole Johnson has leaked the CD to the press. He probably sold it to them for millions of dollars. Damn! This is a disaster! Get my wife in here, and tell all of the news people who call that I'm in a meeting and I'll call them back later."

"Josephine ran out of the president's office and down to his wife's office, leaving all of the press people on hold. She knocked on the door and, this time, Josephine waited to be asked in. She told the First Lady what had happened and that her husband wanted to see her. When Rhonda arrived at the president's office, she could see that her husband was very agitated.

"Rhonda, that son-of-a-bitch Johnson has killed all of my plans for a second term. Oh shit, I'm dead in the water. What am I going to do?"

"I'll tell you what you're going to do. You're going to deny it. Your position is that the CD is a fake put out by the Republican Party, and if Johnson dares to show his face, you'll accuse him of being in league with the Republicans. You can even say he made the fake CD and tried to blackmail you into paying him not to publish it."

"Come on, Rhonda. Those newspapers will be able to authenticate the CD and you can be certain that the Israelis will have some big expert who can authenticate it. Certainly the Jews, whose contributions and votes I need, won't believe me. I've lost them and the race."

"You have nothing to lose. Deny it!"

President Rock finally agreed to simply deny the authenticity of the CD. Rhonda tried to fill him with self-confidence, but she knew it was a longshot even though it was the only shot they had. She felt as down as he did, but this was not the time to let the president know that. Right now, she needed to pick him up so that he could sound as if he was telling the truth when he dealt with the media.

Chapter 45

The Jerusalem Post morning headline read: "President Out to Destroy Israel." The underlying front page story included a full quote of Rock's speech from the CD, but it made no mention of the source of the quote. Individual newspapers handled the story in their own ways. Conservative papers announced the CD with huge headlines, long stories, and questions including how an American President could get involved in such a plot against an ally of the United States. Likewise, conservative leaning TV stations quickly created entire shows, with street interviews, about the effect of the CD on future United States relations with countries all over the world. Each paper and station stated that it had a copy of the CD and that the CD had been authenticated as unaltered.

Liberal newspapers either refused to carry the story or placed it on back pages. Some simply announced that they wouldn't print it until the president responded to it. Liberal leaning TV shows followed the lead of the liberal newspapers. Finally, President Rock appeared on nationwide TV and claimed that the CD was a forgery and no such meeting had ever happened. He refused to answer questions, but he stated his undying support of Israel. In Israel, their expert watched Rock's televised press conference and concluded it was clear that President Rock was lying. That was no surprise since another government expert had already proclaimed the CD to be authentic.

The international media treatment of the story was mixed. The media of most western countries carried the story without comment. Most governments declined to comment. The Russians stated that the United States had often accused other governments of doing bad things, and now the President of the United States had stuck his foot in a bunch of do-do. All of the Middle East governments involved in the president's plan denied that the meeting described in the CD had ever taken place. Hamas, Iran, and Syria accused Israel of creating a fake CD to force Rock out of office so that Israel could manipulate the United States presidential election for its own benefit. All of them ignored the fact that the CD was genuine.

Republican presidential candidate Leo Short put out newspaper and TV ads reporting that he had several laboratories analyze the CD and that all of them found it to be authentic. He heavily criticized President Rock for planning to destroy an ally of the United States. Rock countered by accusing Short of political sensationalism.

The battle lines were now clearly drawn between Rock's backers and his detractors, with the former simply ignoring the proven authenticity of the CD. In all of the furor, no mention of the name Robert Johnson ever occurred, and only the Israeli government knew that Johnson was living in Israel under the name Cecil Isaacs. Cecil just watched the drama play out daily on TV.

Chapter 46

Several months later, as the election was drawing near, both the Democrats and the Republicans ordered independent analyses of campaign contributions and voter trends. Around the same time, the Israeli government also commissioned the same study. In addition, the Israeli government made a study of American Jewish presidential campaign donors and the candidate Jewish voters were most likely to support.

All three studies showed the same startling result: Jewish contributions to President Rock were only slightly below estimates made before the public airing of the damning CD, and Jewish voters still overwhelmingly backed Rock. Furthermore, backed by Jewish campaign contributions and probable Jewish votes, Rock was projected to win re-election.

Leo Short viewed the results in a state of disbelief. It was impossible for him to comprehend that the very Jews who had prayed for a Jewish homeland for centuries and had only gotten one because of the murder of six million Jews by the nazis during World War II were willing to give President Rock the benefit of the doubt against a CD proven accurate that Rock intended to destroy Israel if he is re-elected. If the Jews were wrong about Rock, and all of the evidence showed that they were wrong, then they were destroying their own hopes for a Jewish homeland. Short simply couldn't comprehend that they would take that risk.

As Leo Short leaned back in his chair, all he could say to his campaign manager was: "Like Hitler was, Rock is an expert at the 'big lie.' The 'big lie' is when you tell a lie that is so fantastic people believe it because they can't believe anyone could make up something that incredible. That's the only reason I can think of why people would believe Rock's story that the CD is a fake even though independent laboratories confirm that it's real."

Across town, at the White House, President and Mrs. Rock also could hardly believe the information they had just received; however, they were celebrating. The president and his wife were laughing uproariously and were toasting each other with very expensive wine paid for by the taxpayers.

"Rhonda, nothing is too good for us today. You were right. All I had to do is say the CD was a fake and people believed me."

"I told you it would work. Don't I always know best? Haven't I always known what is best for you since we met?"

"Of course. That's why I married you, that and because I love you. The Jews believe me in spite of all the evidence that I'm trying to destroy Israel. Isn't that incredible?"

Chapter 47

In Israel, the Prime Minister met with his Cabinet in emergency session and explained the information he had just received about the American presidential election.

The Cabinet members sat in silence as they received the news. After reading the report, the Prime Minister looked up and, in a grave tone of voice, said:

"President Rock will probably win re-election using Jewish contributions and Jewish votes. It's very ironic, isn't it? I suppose it's much like the Jewish world is committing suicide. It seems as if the American Jews have learned nothing from the Holocaust.

"The only thing we can do now is begin planning for an all-out war to the death within a year."

THE END

CPSIA information can be obtained at www.ICGtesting.com
Printed in the USA
LVOW070558081012

301850LV00005B/4/P